SWORN VIRGIN

SWORN VIRGIN

Elvira Dones

Translated by
Clarissa Botsford

Foreword by Ismail Kadare

LONDON · NEW YORK

First published in English translation in 2014 by
And Other Stories
London – New York

www.andotherstories.org

First published as *Vergine giurata* in October 2007 by Giangiacomo Feltrinelli Editore, Milan, Italy

ISBN 9781908276346
eBook ISBN 9781908276353

A catalogue record for this book is available from the British Library.

The translation of this book was made possible by the receipt in 2011 of a PEN/Heim Translation Fund Grant from the Pen American Center.

This book has been selected to receive financial assistance from English PEN's Writers in Translation programme supported by Bloomberg. English PEN exists to promote literature and its understanding, uphold writers' freedoms around the world, campaign against the persecution and imprisonment of writers for stating their views, and promote the friendly co-operation of writers and free exchange of ideas.

To my daughter Iuna

FOREWORD

Elvira Dones is one of the most distinguished Albanian authors writing today. Astonishing, brilliant, and unabashed by taboos of any kind, she is as much at ease in Albanian as in the rest of European literature. This is not only because she writes in two languages – Albanian and Italian (a tradition that goes back to the late middle ages, when the Ottomans prohibited written Albanian and our writers used Latin as a second language) – but because her vision of art and of the world is in harmony with both Albanian and European culture.

Her novel *Sworn Virgin* takes an apparently exotic subject, but one drawing on literature's oldest archetypes: the creation of a double, and the transformation of a human being. Hana, the attractive young woman who is the protagonist of this novel, agrees of her own free will to 'turn into a man.'

The story refers to an ancient if rare Albanian custom that has been preserved into the modern era, according to which, for various reasons – such as the absence of a man in a household or, as in Hana's case, the fear of rape – a 'conversion' was permitted and a woman could change her status from female to male. She would gain all a man's rights and freedoms, adopt male behavior and dress, take part in assemblies of elders, and go out to cafés to drink alcohol and smoke cigarettes, with the sole condition that she preserve her virginity.

This apparently paradoxical and anomalous custom also has a surreal dimension: it presents a loss as a privilege, and offers subjection in the guise of freedom.

The protagonist of this novel passes through all the tribulations of this frightening transformation like the actor in some extraordinary role in a classical drama that hurtles towards its dénouement.

Ismail Kadare
Translated by John Hodgson
September 2013

The vast, infinite life will begin all over again,
a life not seeing, not talking, not thinking.

From 'Quatrains'
by Nâzim Hikmet[1]

OCTOBER 2001

'So, Mr Doda, you're a poet,' says her traveling companion, who has occupied the seat next to Hana on the plane for the last seven hours.

The line of passengers waiting to get through passport control at Washington International Airport snakes tiredly.

'Not really.' She tries to smile.

'But you write poems, if I've understood you correctly.'

You can't write good poems with a dry cunt, she says in her head. She looks away. A woman is touching up her lipstick, her husband watching with slight disgust, tapping his fingers on his passport. Hana catalogs the scene under the heading: 'Man out of love, woman still hopeful, marriage ceasefire about to expire.'

You can't write good poems with a dry cunt, she thinks to herself again, annoyed. Why the hell did she tell him she wrote? He pins her down with his look. It's no good, she thinks, your enlightened male brain will never be able to guess. Hana smoothes down her man's suit. The sports jacket is a bit big, but not too much.

Her traveling companion stared at her in the same way during the flight.

'Here's my card,' he now says. 'In case you need anything, information about the capital, any suggestions. If I'm not traveling around the world or at my house in Geneva, I'll be in DC. Seriously, call me whenever you want, Mr Doda. I'd be happy to help out.'

Mark concentrates on his carry-on. On his shoes. On his cell phone, which he wants to turn on. I'm sorry, she pleads in silence. Hana reads the name on the card: Patrick O'Connor. The man is of Irish origin. She smiles. Christ, we country folk can sniff each other out.

Her left breast begins to itch. She tries to scratch herself without using her hand. She started feeling the presence of her breasts a year ago, as soon as she got her green card and decided to emigrate to America. She can't seem to stop the itching.

'Mr Doda,' Patrick O'Connor calls, indicating with a nod of his head the passport controller's narrow cubicle.

The line has moved on. Hana kicks her bag forward. Her brown shoes, one on either side of the bag, look like little hibernating bears.

'What is the purpose of your visit to the United States, Ms Doda?' the officer asks as he opens her passport.

It's too late to go back now. Even the village knows he left holding the passport of a woman.

The village had observed, with penetrating, attentive eyes. The way he was dressed on the day he said goodbye was the object of quiet scrutiny; there were no comments. It was a dark time, and people had little energy to spare. Past glory had faded into the howls and excrement of stray dogs. Shreds of history; the moans of gangsters whose only law was the code of honor; suns that were afraid to set for fear of being surprised by death.

Patrick O'Connor – impatient now, the rhythm of everyday life suddenly printed on his face – holds out his hand.

'It was a real pleasure talking with you. Too bad you don't have a phone number here in the US yet. Maybe we can talk again before I go back to Albania. Look me up if you want, I really mean it. Well, good luck.'

Hana shakes his hand shyly. She's a little sorry they're parting ways. For seven hours this man was her safety net. O'Connor spent part of the time tapping on the keyboard of a sleek white computer with a picture of a bitten apple on its top. What a beautiful object, she had thought. Then he started talking. He was a great conversation-maker, not at all formal.

'Use that phone number, really!' O'Connor shouts for the last time, as he turns to leave. 'I'm pretty sure you'll need it.'

She gets through the first stage of passport control and breathes a sigh of relief. They point her to an office where she has to go through more formalities. A half-empty room with thin plaster walls. With her limited vocabulary she finds it hard to assemble answers to the officer's questions, but the man is patient, and Hana is grateful to him.

'Welcome to the United States of America, Ms Doda,' he says at last. 'That's all we need to know. You can go now.'

She runs into the nearest men's room, catapulting herself towards a washbasin. The face in the mirror is angular. Hana shifts her gaze to a man waiting to go into one of the stalls. Others, unabashed and hasty, relieve themselves at the urinals. The door opens and closes to the irregular beat of the travelers' footsteps.

Hana takes a deep breath, hoping to tame her panic. The family is waiting at Arrivals. There's her cousin Lila, her thirteen-year-old niece Jonida – whom Hana hasn't seen since she was a baby – and their husband and father Shtjefën, as well as some other people from the village who emigrated years before. 'Proud to be American,' as they had said in their badly written letters. They've come from various places in Maryland, and from Virginia and Pennsylvania, and even from Ohio.

Hana had spent a great deal of time poring over a map of the United States, but her imagination had melted at the sheer size of the country. America is immense. She had been living in a village of 280 people.

Out! Now! She says to herself almost aloud. Get out and be a man.

That's what the clan expects. They want to see what they left behind, a young man gone gray with the weight of duty, a much-loved relative but an oddball. Mark's arrival is meant to bring them back to the mountains, to the smell of dung, to the splutter of guns, to betrayal, songs, wounds, flowers, to brutality, to the seduction of the mountain trails inviting them to throw themselves over the edge, to love.

Hana shakes her thoughts away. This restroom in Dulles International Airport is so real and tangible, and yet she feels so alien here. You need balls to deal with all this, she thinks, balls she doesn't have. And that's not all you need. Why balls? Why? Why me?

Get out of this bathroom, she tells herself. Get out of here, for Christ's sake!

'Do you need anything, sir?' asks a voice to her left.

She turns around. It's a boy of about fourteen. Or even fifteen, or sixteen.

'Are you feeling ok?' he persists, in an accent that sounds familiar to her.

Hana swallows, smiles, straightens up from the washbasin. Says she's fine, thanks. Almost apologizing.

The boy looks at her, not as self-assured as before. A man – it must be his father, the resemblance is uncanny – comes out of one of the stalls, approaches his son and rests his hand on his shoulder.

'Is everything all right, Hikmet?'

The boy's face doesn't look at all Turkish, or Arabic; he's almost blond. The father, on the other hand, has a polished face but dark, marked features.

'This man isn't feeling well,' says Hikmet.

Hana denies this, shaking her head, and says, 'Hikmet? That's a beautiful name. Turkish, right?'

The man doesn't seem concerned that the stranger is feeling unwell.

'How do you know?'

'I'm Albanian.'

The man pauses a moment, granting a sliver of transient trust to the word Albanian, before doubt returns.

'*Arnavut,*' he says, looking for confirmation in Turkish.

'Albanian,' Hana repeats.

'We live in London. I often come to the States on business and this time I brought Hikmet with me.'

She doesn't know what to say. Her poor English paralyzes her. The boy is almost at the door.

'So, you are feeling better,' states the man, dropping the question mark.

Hana nods.

'Good luck.'

'You also.'

Father and son exit.

More time passes before she decides to face her

family. She emerges from the restroom like a man on death row, like a fool in a flash of lucidity.

Arms are waving in the air; she hears a girl's voice shout, 'Uncle Maaaaark!' Out of the corner of her eye she glimpses the threatening tail of a German Shepherd on a leash, held by a man in uniform. Her cousin Lila throws herself into her arms. There is much agitation.

'Hello, cousin!' Lila cries. 'Here we all are. But where were you? Where were you? We thought you'd been sent back.'

'Why would they do that?'

'How should I know? All the passengers from Zurich came out ages ago.'

'*Tungjatë, bre burrë.*'* Shtjefën Dibra, Lila's husband, greets her with an energetic embrace.

'*Tungjatë*, Shtjefën.'

'Uncle Mark! I'm Jonida, do you recognize me?'

'Jonida, you're so big now!'

They order coffee, which is served in plastic cups. The coffee is sad, tasting vaguely like rainwater.

She's had coffee like this in Scutari a couple of times, where the barmen save money on coffee grounds: one day you might get supplies from the other side of the border,

---

*   'Well, man, how are you?' (A greeting typically heard in northern Albania.)

from Montenegro or Kosovo, and the next day you might not. In Tirana, the capital, you can get hold of most things, but Tirana is remote and hard to think about.

Jonida pierces Hana with her look. She sucks on her orange juice, making too much noise, and is scolded by Lila.

'Uncle Mark, now I get it,' she says at last.

'What?'

'That you're totally weird.'

'Oh yes?' Hana smiles. Lila shakes her head as if to say sorry. Shtjefën looks awkward.

'Yeah, weird.' The girl's attack continues. 'I mean, like, your clothes look borrowed. Nobody in America wears stuff like that. And you don't have a beard.'

'Jonida, shut up,' Lila implores. 'What are you doing? I begged you to behave yourself . . . '

'If you keep busting your uncle's balls, he'll turn right around and go back to Albania,' threatens Shtjefën, without much conviction.

Jonida starts laughing, shrugging her shoulders, free and stubborn. One of the relatives, Pal, belches noisily; his wife Sanìja's cell phone rings.

'He can't go anywhere,' the young girl argues. 'And stop being such a know-it-all, Dad. How's he going to go back with no money? The ticket costs like . . . '

She's still laughing. Two amazing dimples in her cheeks. She's beautiful, so different from the way Hana had imagined her.

'Tell me, Uncle Mark – you don't have the money to go back, right?'

'That is right.'

'And Scutari is the ugliest place in the world, right?'

'That is also true.'

'And half of the village has emigrated like us, right?'

'Yes, that is true too.'

'The north is the poorest part of Albania, right?'

'Unfortunately.'

'And you don't have a beard, right?'

Sanìja gets up and moves away to finish her phone call. Lila blushes. Shtjefën is furious. Pal looks down awkwardly at his chewed nails. Cousin Nikolìn and his wife Rudina freeze to the spot.

Hana tries to change the subject. 'So you know quite a bit about your country?'

'The internet. Do you know what the internet is?'

'A little, yes.'

'But you really don't have a beard!'

'No, I don't.'

The women stare blatantly, in silence. Lila smiles and murmurs words of encouragement to her cousin but avoids saying her name, though on the phone and in her letters she has always called her 'Dear sister Hana.'

Hana feels calm now. She doesn't mind her family; it was the limbo of expectation that made her feel sick.

'At home I've made chicken pilaf and a chocolate cake,' Lila whispers in her ear. 'It's typical American food,' she adds proudly.

She expects Hana to be impressed, but Hana can only mutter, 'Oh yes, that's good.'

'You'll be sleeping in the kitchen, Uncle Mark,' Jonida informs her. 'So every time Dad gets up to smoke or have a snack he'll wake you up.'

'Yes, Shtjefën keeps strange hours. Sometimes he goes to work at three or four in the morning. It's bad, so he can't sleep like regular people and he gets up to smoke or eat. You know, at home things are a bit cramped – I already told you on the phone, right? But don't you worry about a thing.'

How do I look to her? Hana wonders, stubbing out her cigarette. She observes mother and daughter; they don't look at all alike. Lila has gained some weight, but her face is still pretty. She's a natural blond, her eyes are a limpid blue, she's tall and solid, her teeth are wrecked like most Albanians'. Jonida's gaze is dark but warm, her hair long and parted down the middle, her eyebrows curved and bushy. Big mouth, straight nose and a really beautiful forehead.

'So, Mark, why don't we go, brother?' Shtjefën suggests. 'It takes over an hour to get home with the traffic the way it is, and you must be jet-lagged. And it's almost dinner time.'

'It's up to you. I don't know.'

'Anyway, we'll see you next Sunday for a dinner you won't forget,' says Pal. 'Today was just to welcome you, now we really should . . .'

Under the communists, Pal was the elementary-school teacher in the village. Something in his voice has stayed nasal and pedantic. This is the first time Hana has seen Sanìja and Rudina, the cousins' wives. Of course, they must know the whole story and be dying to fire questions at her, like rounds from a semi-automatic; but they realize that it's not the right time or place.

Hana can't take her eyes off Jonida. The girl winks at her.

'Uncle Mark,' she concludes as she gets up, 'you're the funniest guy I've ever met.'

'Jonida!' shouts Shtjefën. 'From now till we get to the house you keep that mouth of yours shut!'

'Yes, Dad.'

'That's an order, in case you haven't got the message.'

'It was clear, Shtjefën,' says Lila, trying to smooth things over.

'Sorry, Dad.'

'It's your uncle you should apologize to, not me.'

'Sorry, Uncle.'

•

'Forgive me, Uncle Gjergj,' Hana had implored. 'I beg you.'

Without lifting his head, he had only grunted, like a bear. Then he had shouted, 'Get out!'

She had left the room shaking. Forgive me, she had implored again to herself, without even knowing why she was begging forgiveness.

The others go. The men take their leave in the typical style of the north, pressing their foreheads together for a second, left hand on Hana's shoulder, solemnly pronouncing the formula: 'May you remain in good health, man.' Then the Dibras leave too, with Hana in tow.

The journey to the house is tense, like a rifle shot waiting to be fired. Hana sits in the back of the car, next to Jonida, despite Lila's efforts to make her sit in front. Shtjefën drives well, fast and attentive, a dancer on four wheels in a five-lane highway with cars passing on both sides. But he is tenser than he was at the airport.

'The Beltway is always stressful,' he comments, handing Hana a cigarette. She takes it but does not light up.

Every now and then Lila turns and smiles. Jonida stares out of the window, music playing to her through earphones and isolating her from the rest of the world, while the movement of the knee on which her CD player rests marks the rhythm of her temporary sojourn in another dimension.

The sunset is incredible, like a blood orange. Hana understands only that they are traveling northeast, leaving the capital behind them. The interstate signs flash past like prison runaways in green-and-white uniforms.

Jonida drums on her knee. Hana sees her hand holding out a note written in block letters:

YOUR ENGLISH SUCKS. I'LL TEACH YOU AMERICAN. YOU CAN COUNT ON IT.

Shtjefën and Jonida have already gone to bed.

'Here we are, alone at last,' says Lila.

Hana looks at her affectionately. Her breast is still itching. Lila is incredibly tense. May God help us, thinks Hana. It can't be easy; she wouldn't like to be in Lila's place right now.

'Listen,' Hana says invitingly, 'why don't we relax a bit, both of us?'

Lila perches on a stool, making her look even more vulnerable.

'I want you to feel comfortable.'

'Really?'

'Yes, really, Lila.'

Lila hugs her abruptly, kneeling down in front of her. Hana feels lost in her embrace, ill at ease. Lila understands and breaks away from her, returning to her stool. The grating metallic sound of a passing train drowns out the awkwardness of the moment, reducing the tension.

'No drama. Ok, I get it,' says Lila. 'And no more hugs.'

Hana thinks about it. She lights a cigarette. She feels suddenly exposed and ugly.

'No, hugs are ok,' she murmurs. 'Every now and then. I think they might do me good.'

'D'you want to go to bed?' Lila says, changing the subject. 'It's past midnight and you must be beat, it's six in the morning for you.'

'No, I'm not sleepy.'

'I am.'

'You go then.'

'No.'

Lila takes a cigarette from Hana's pack and lights it. From the room next door they can hear Shtjefën's rhythmic snoring.

'He's a good man, right?' Hana asks.

'Yes, he's a good father, and always tries to be a good husband.'

Lila puts the fruit bowl in the middle of the table. She starts to pull grapes off the bunch and, rather than eating them, she arranges them in a row on the table.

'How did you live alone all these years?'

Hana lets the minutes go by. 'I wasn't alone,' she answers. 'If anything, the opposite.'

'What do you mean?'

Hana does not shift her gaze from the row of grapes.

'Have you forgotten the mountains, Lila?'

'The mountains?'

'Yes. Mountains made of eyes that observe and forbid, mountains made of silence . . . '

Shtjefën stops snoring. Hana eats the first grape in the chain. The tablecloth is so white. The kitchen is reassuringly spick and span. Lila, sitting in front of her, is a stranger.

'It would have been easier if I'd been alone,' she says.

Her man's sports jacket has been shed in the corner. All evening, nobody has dared to pick it up and put it away.

'Do you want me to peel an apple for you?' Lila offers.

Hana bursts out laughing. It's a kind laugh, one that nurtures itself and keeps itself going. She gets up, straightens her shoulders and adjusts her baggy pants.

'Stop treating me like a man who needs to be served! I'm just your cousin Hana, we're the same age and you're letting me stay in your apartment,' she says, not holding back her laughter. 'I can do things for myself.'

'What's the matter?'

'I'm laughing.'

'Why?'

'I thought I was ready to take this step, but now I'm scared stiff . . . and so are you. That's why I'm laughing.'

'You really are weird.' Lila runs her hand through her hair. 'You always were. Were you like this even as a man?'

'As a man I carried a rifle, drove a truck and was careful with my words. But what do you know? You had already gone to America.'

'Can I hug you again?'

Hana doesn't answer. They embrace with a slow and harmonious gesture and stay entwined naturally. Hana's head barely reaches Lila's shoulder.

'You need to take off these men's clothes.'

'There's no hurry.'

'The sooner you get rid of them the better.'

'That's not true.'

'I thought that was the deal. That you were coming here to go back to what you were.'

'Yes, but there's no hurry.'

Lila detaches herself and stares straight into her eyes. Hana smiles.

'I'm in no hurry. And anyway, that's not the most important thing.'

Her cousin is confused. Hana leans towards her and pulls the hair back from Lila's face.

'Jonida's more important. I thought you had told her.'

Shtjefën appears at the door, pale and imposing in his light-blue pajamas.

'Are you still up? . . . I'm thirsty.'

He goes to the fridge, pulls out a bottle, and drinks.

'Sorry, I'm going back to bed.'

Suddenly Lila is overwhelmed by tiredness.

'I can't take any more, let's go to bed too.'

'I was talking to you about Jonida.'

'I was never any good at explaining things to her,' Lila says. 'Around her I'm just a bundle of emotions. Shtjefën didn't know what to do either. Then we both agreed. Who knows? If the Americans play some nasty trick on Hana and don't let her into the country, there's no point in upsetting the girl.'

'Why wouldn't they let me in?'

'What planet are you from, Hana? A month ago it was the end of the world here.' She crosses herself. 'Security measures, fear of other attacks . . . all those things.'

Hana picks up her jacket and caresses it slowly.

'We heard about September 11th, even over there,' she says resentfully. 'Even up in the mountains we have TV, what did you think?'

Lila laughs and puts the fruit bowl back in the fridge.

'What's wrong? You're acting all offended now. I know you have TV, but it's another world over there.'

Hana looks out of the window. It'll soon be dawn. Opposite there are two buildings; down below, rows of parked cars.

'Yes, we saw everything on the TV in the Rrnajë bar, but that day we'd drunk too much raki because Frrok had just married off his daughter, and the television was half broken, the sound wasn't working.'

The idea of lying down on the bed is inviting, Hana thinks. What is the village doing now? What is every one of its 280 inhabitants thinking at this precise moment?

'Come on, bedtime! I'm dying,' orders Lila.

'I feel tender,' Hana says.

The stones in the river at Rrnajë looked like foam. She had observed them, in her meticulous and disciplined way. Then she had understood. They looked like foam because they were white, too white at times, when water danced over them in a fury. Hana didn't like fury: it tarnished her peace. Even the mountains' name left her ambivalent: Bjeshkët e Namuna, the 'cursed mountains.' The name was too definitive; it left so little room for hope. And yet, close up, the mountains were tame, you just needed to know how to take them. You just needed to learn to sleep there without thinking of the name, a name made up by an outsider, some traveler who knew nothing about the place. There's no curse, just caution and silence. If you don't attack them, the mountains, they'll leave you alone.

She wakes at one in the afternoon and stays in bed a little longer. Then she gets up and looks furtively down the narrow hallway. The apartment smells of lemon, sugar, and coffee. Her imitation Samsonite suitcase, bought in the bazaar behind the great mosque in Scutari, has disappeared, and so have Shtjefën's shoes.

Lila comes out of the bathroom, smiling and busy. Hana pauses and pats the top of her head, suddenly feeling naked.

'Good morning!' Lila greets her. 'Why are you patting your hair?'

'I dreamed they were shaving my hair off on sheep-shearing day.'

Lila laughs hesitantly to start with, then her laugh grows, in a crescendo she doesn't hold back. Hana follows suit, comfortable in her funny baggy pajamas. Lila goes on laughing, and then she pushes Hana into the living room. On the table there's a feast. Hana decides she must first stop in the bathroom, where a new toothbrush and tube of toothpaste await her, together with various little bottles and unfamiliar paraphernalia. Beautiful towels. She stares at them at length; she's afraid to use them, she doesn't want to ruin them.

A year before, back at the village, Maria had received six towels like these from her daughter, who had emigrated to Italy. She had sewn them together and made curtains for the guest room. They were nice curtains: they went well with the rifles hanging in a row along the wall. Ten generations of the Frangaj family men ranged across the wall. No male voice had been heard in that house for a decade, since the blood feud had taken away the last of the Frangaj men, Maria's son. If she had accepted the offers made by foreigners passing through the mountains after the communists fell she could have made a fortune selling those rifles. But she never had.

She washes quickly and comes out of the bathroom with her face still wet. Lila is pouring the coffee. Hana decides to light up a cigarette. They sit in silence.

Now, in the daylight, the apartment looks beautiful.

'They say that you've been getting stranger and stranger,' Lila says, more to herself than to her cousin. 'They say you spend your time writing and reading.'

Greenish smoke plays around Lila's curls.

'Does that scare you, Lila? I mean, the fact that I'm weird?'

Lila doesn't say a word.

'I took the animals out, I chopped the wood, I worked in the fields, I went to the village meetings and I drank a lot of raki. Nothing else counts.'

'But this morning, who are you?' Lila asks cautiously. 'Have you decided to be Hana or Mark?'

Whatever happened the day after her arrival, Hana had promised herself she would not regret it. She had never regretted anything and she wasn't about to start now, at the age of thirty-four.

'For you, I'm Hana. For the others I'll still be Mark for a while.'

'Ok.'

'Ok what?'

'You're Mark. I have to treat you like a man.'

'I told you that for you I'm the same old Hana. Yesterday that's what you called me. What's making you change your mind?'

Lila explains that this morning she looks like a man: her dark skin, her morning hair, those baggy pajamas, her yellow teeth, her masculine gestures. She finds it hard to think of her as a woman. Hana plays for time. It's strange, but hearing those words hurts. On the table there are those buns with a hole in the middle, three little jam jars, butter, orange juice, coffee, sugar, hard-boiled eggs. Stop making an inventory, she tells herself.

'I've been a man for fourteen years.'

Lila tries to drown her gaze in the oily dregs of the coffee.

'It's not going to be easy,' she says finally. 'Not for any of us.'

'Really?' Hana says, with a hint of a smile. 'I didn't know that.'

'Don't start now. You're the one with the education here. I just say what comes into my head.'

Lila checks the clock on the wall impatiently. It's nearly two o'clock.

'I'm as ignorant as an ameba,' Hana says. 'Education is a big word.'

'Well, you went to college, didn't you?'

'Yeah, but only for a year, before going up into the mountains and becoming a man.'

'Well, I'm a cleaning lady, my dear.'

'You were the top student in high school.'

Lila starts laughing. 'And you're the biggest liar in the northern hemisphere.'

Hana can't seem to change gear. The pain is rising up inside her. She tries to react, taking ten long breaths. With every breath she feels the tension dissipate. But it's not enough. Lila looks at her maternally.

'Did I really use to tell lies?'

'You bet. Any excuse and you were off making up some story or other. We would mention some guy's name, and you'd start with some tall tale about him.'

'There was no TV then. Somebody had to be the entertainer. Those were the days,' Hana sighs, with a smile.

'Except we were all practically engaged by then,' Lila contradicts, spreading butter on those strange buns after carefully slicing them in half. Her fingers are odd; they're too long and thin for her stocky body.

'Bagel,' she says, like a nursery schoolteacher. 'They're called bagels. They're good. Try one.'

Lila spreads butter on one half, drips some honey on it, and takes a bite.

'The truth is, you had a hell of a great time spinning those stories,' Lila picks up from where she left off. 'You got pleasure out of it, your face lit up, you could have gone on for hours.'

Hana imitates Lila, slicing the bagel, spreading the butter, trickling the honey, taking a bite.

'Now I have to invent my own life,' she announces when the bagel is finished.

'Let's start today. We've a lot to do. You've already wasted enough time.'

'No, today no. It's too soon.'

'Jonida will be home from school any minute. School's out at three, and the bus brings her home.'

'How am I supposed to behave with her?'

'Just be Mark. Or else, tell her everything.'

'I think you're right. Today it's best if I'm still her uncle. Then we'll see.'

'Now, go take a shower. Do you have a change of clothes?'

She has everything, except the chance to get away from her own silence. Now she's in Rockville, a suburb of Washington, DC. She can't be rude. She can't shut herself up in a room of her own and play around with poems of the past and the present. The dead are best. They don't create problems for you. They don't laugh in your face.

The dead are polite. *Goodbye, my brother sea.*[2] She suddenly thinks about the Turkish boy in the men's room at the airport. She wonders whether he's ever read a poem by Hikmet, his namesake. She misses Hikmet. Recently he's been a friend, mixed in with a bit of Seamus Heaney and a bit of Pablo Neruda. Be normal, people say.

'When are you going back to work, Lila?'

'In three days . . . You're not getting rid of me before that, you better believe it. Then for three more days Shtjefën will stay at home with you, and after that you'll have to take care of yourself because you'll be on your own at home. Now go and take that shower and freshen up – Jonida's on her way.'

Later, while she's taking a walk with her cousin and niece, Hana breathes in the afternoon air. The park is alive with brilliant colors. Hordes of mothers with strollers and children, their shouts in a multitude of languages helping Hana go by undetected.

Lila, not without pride, explains that this is a good area to live in. Sure, the houses are more expensive, and that's why they've had to make do with such a small apartment. But a walk in the park is better than ten diets and three sessions in a beauty parlor. Hana thrusts her hands into the pockets of her pants and looks like any man in the street.

Jonida skips in front of them and chats about this and that, mixing Albanian Gheg with American English.[3]

She tells them about something she does at school called 'social studies,' and about her teacher, who talks too much and can't keep the class quiet. 'He's a dickhead,' she says three times, enough for Hana to learn a new word.

'Uncle Mark, you look good in that white shirt, but I thought you'd be bigger. In the photo you look bigger, you know? You really have to tell me about the mountains. I need to know everything. Mom never tells me anything. Neither does Dad. They're too busy working all day.'

'If we don't work then who's going to feed you, sweetie?' says Lila. The girl isn't listening. She's doing pirouettes. She's like a gazelle, a comet, a love poem. She's wearing tight-fitting, low-cut jeans, her belly button showing, a blue t-shirt with white writing on it, and underneath a red bra with thin shoulder straps just showing.

'Do I look good, Uncle Mark?'

'You're beautiful.'

'I want you to like me since Mom really likes you. She's been talking about you so much with Dad these past months, and all Dad said was "Yes, yes, yes . . . "' She mimics Shtjefën's voice. 'There's a secret, right?' Hana doesn't answer. 'I have to find out the secret. If we're friends you'll tell me everything, won't you?'

Lila has stopped. Hana is stuck halfway between Jonida and her mother.

'What's this place called?' Hana asks.

'Don't try and change the subject.'

'What's it called?'

'Rockville. It's called Rockville. But don't try and be clever. Are you going to tell me everything about you?'

'Of course.'

'And about the mountains?'

'Whatever you want.'

'Great! I can't wait for the old folks to get back to work so I can have you all to myself after school.'

Hana laughs. Jonida rushes on ahead to say hi to a gang of friends.

'Calm down, Hana. Relax,' Lila whispers affectionately.

'I'm very relaxed, I promise.'

The evening with Shtjefën isn't as bad as she feared. He's so tired that he doesn't even take a shower before sitting down to eat. He says sorry a few times; he smells like highways and tar. His eyes are glazed and he talks more slowly than the night before. His voice is like gravel. He asks three times what the two women in his life have done today and if, by any chance, they have had time to think. 'Of course we have, dear!' Lila reassures him. 'Of course you have,' Shtjefën echoes. He's part bear, part butterfly, this man. He goes on slurping his bean soup. 'What about you, Mark? Did you get some rest? You look a bit lost, brother.' Hana doesn't answer. She holds on to her spoon and can't decide whether she's hungry or not. What's for sure is that she doesn't want to talk. She takes in the atmosphere: the gestures that warm the air, the rhythmic tapping of Jonida's foot under the table, the shouts from the neighborhood children wafting through the open window, the uncertain dance of the drawn-back curtain.

Before asking for Lila's hand, Shtjefën had been wiry and blond. His head was like a sunflower. The girls in the village said it was because of his height: he caught the sun as soon as it came out, long before the others, and was the last to lose it before sundown. His speech sounded rare and distant, like the glory that cloaked his family. The Dibras had been a great *fis*, a family clan that had been at war with the Turks for centuries. After the fall of the Ottoman Empire, the mountains had enjoyed a brief peace. But then the communists had come, decreed the downfall of the *fis* and executed their leaders, the *bajraktar*.

But that is the past and history is no longer important.

In the next-door apartment they're still cooking. The clanging of saucepans mixed with children's voices and spicy smells make her feel like she's part of a giant communal soup kitchen.

'Our neighbors are from Sri Lanka,' Jonida explains. She smirks: 'They have six kids.'

'Did school go ok, sweetie?' Shtjefën asks.

'As smooth as anything, Dad.'

'Good girl.'

'And you?'

'Me what?'

'How did work go?'

'There's a lot of it, and as long as there's a lot of it, I'm taking it, my little girl. If my boss knew how to organize things, it'd be even better. That guy's a mess.'

'Oh no, God save us,' Jonida laughs. 'Don't start on the story of your boss, *please*.'

Shtjefën doesn't take it hard; he shakes his head and shifts the soup bowl to one side. Lila's fighting with the mashed potato and the *qofte* meatballs.

'Now Mom and I have two men in the house, we need to rewrite the rules of household management,' Jonida decrees.

Mother and father exchange smiles.

'We're in a phase of full-blown feminism here,' Shtjefën tells Hana. 'Since our daughter does absolutely nothing at home, she's championing women's rights.'

'I do a lot, Dad,' Jonida says as she attacks a meatball. 'You're never home so you never see, that's all.'

Lila serves the other adults. Shtjefën pours some grappa for himself and for Hana.

'Right,' Shtjefën says. 'Tell me what you do, smarty-pants.'

Jonida lifts her hair up behind her neck, then drops it, rolls her eyes to give herself an air of importance, and then rests her elbows on the table.

'I'm your muse: I inspire you, I breathe life into you.'

The adults laugh.

Dinner is soon over and there is an atmosphere of tenderness. Hana offers to do the dishes.

'Since when do men wash dishes?' Jonida jokes.

Lila says, 'No way, Hana.'

'Look, all these years I've been doing everything around the house,' Hana says, trying to convince them. 'I know how to do women's work.' But Lila is adamant.

Shtjefën lights a cigarette.

'Tomorrow after school, let's go out just you and me, Uncle Mark,' Jonida says, before going to bed. 'I want you to meet my two best friends who live a block away.'

Hana wants to know why they would want to meet her.

'What? Are you shy or something?' Jonida exclaims. 'If it's a language problem, don't worry – ok? You make yourself perfectly clear.'

'It's not a language problem.'

'So what is it?'

Hana looks at Lila, who shakes her head.

'You three are weird,' the girl comments. 'God only knows what's going on with you.'

'Listen, Jonida,' says Hana, gathering her courage. 'Before meeting your friends, you and I have to talk.'

'Whenever you want. Do you like ice cream?'

Hana nods.

The parents, sitting facing one another, each look at the opposite wall. The young girl looks downcast.

'It's nothing serious, right, Mom?'

'Not serious, no.'

'Nobody's ill or anything?'

'No.'

'Well, nothing else is important,' Jonida continues, relieved. 'So, Uncle Mark, now that you've put this idea in my head, how am I supposed to hold on until tomorrow?'

'There are some things you can't say just like that. Be a little patient.'

'Ok. I'll just go get my school bag ready, then I won't think about it anymore.'

She goes out of the room. Shtjefën is worried and stares at Hana.

'Are you sure you know what you're doing, brother?'

Hana smiles, with a hint of dismay.

'Shtjefën, you're going to have to get used to it sooner or later; you're going to have to call me by my girl's name.'

'It's too soon,' he says. 'Look, sorry, but all my life I've seen you as a man.'

'I know. Let's drink on it, then I'm going to take a walk.'

Shtjefën offers to go with her and Hana doesn't say no. Jonida comes in and out of the kitchen, silently watching them from the corner of her eye. Whining fire sirens and rumbling traffic noises come through the window.

Finally, Jonida wishes them all goodnight and goes to bed. Lila goes with her to her room.

There's nothing we can talk about, nothing that can be put into words easily, Hana thinks later on as she and Shtjefën walk, their cigarettes flashing like fireflies. The night is warm, with a light breeze. There are still joggers out in the park. Cars pass slowly. Shtjefën explains that on small roads like these the speed limit is twenty-five miles per hour, and that the Americans are really strict about these things because this area is a middle-class residential district where people are trying to improve themselves, and so . . . Shtjefën leaves the sentence hanging in the air. Hana lights herself another cigarette, unsure what to do with the stub of the first. In the afternoon, when they had gone on the same walk with Jonida, her niece had told her never to throw them on the ground, because if you do you'll get a fine.

'Here, give it to me,' Shtjefën says. He wraps both stubs up in a paper hankie, which he then stuffs in his pocket.

He rests his arm on her shoulder and then hastily withdraws.

'I'm sorry.'

'What about?'

'It's hard.'

Hana waits. Shtjefën takes his time before saying it's weird, this knot of words that he doesn't know how to get out. He says that in the last nine years the mountains seemed so far away that they didn't really exist for him anymore. And now . . . Now finish the sentence, Hana begs in silence.

'Now you come here to America and I don't know how to explain that basically all this time I've been thinking of you as Mark in the village and at the same time as Lila's favorite cousin. With all the raki you've drunk in your time, Hana. All that raki.'

Hana walks away and Shtjefën does not try to catch up. The distance between them increases.

'With all that raki, Hana Doda, here you are.'

Hana stops and turns round angrily.

'Are you drunk, Shtjefën?'

'No.'

'Well say what you mean, then.'

'This is the way I speak.'

'That's not true. Tell me, are you scared? Did you say I could come just because Lila wanted me to? Do I embarrass you? Tell me the truth.'

She listens to her hostile, aggressive words and thinks that maybe she's the one who is drunk around here.

'Does my presence here make you feel strange?' she asks, sweetly.

Shtjefën's heavy body seems to sway.

'With all the raki you've drunk and all the tobacco you've smoked, your voice still has something feminine about it. Jonida noticed. And anyway, no, I'm not scared of anything, not for me and not for us. But for you this is a hard place. America doesn't give you anything for free.'

Hana laughs at this.

'So you really have forgotten the mountains, Shtjefën. You've forgotten how hard it is.'

Shtjefën thinks about this.

'You're going to tell Jonida everything tomorrow?'

'Don't worry, I'll do it properly.'

'She's growing up so fast that it's hard to keep up. Lila and I work like crazy and we can barely make ends meet. Sometimes I get back from work and Jonida's already in bed, and when we're having breakfast together at the weekend she already has new words in her head. In five years she might be in college, and I'm thinking, God, how am I going to . . . ?'

Hana is getting used to Shtjefën's unfinished sentences.

Back then she didn't know him well. She remembered that a long time ago he was the best dancer in those cursed mountains. Once he had even been sent to the National Folk-dancing Festival at Gjirokastër. His sword dance had won the men's top prize.

Pictures of Shtjefën and the other guy dancing with him used to hang on the 'Socialist Emulation' notice board in the district hall, right in the center of the village. Their arms bearing the glinting swords were thrust up high, their felt skullcaps pushed back, their red and black vests open like wild roses. Hana remembers that it had not been long after the dance that she took the decision to become a man. At Shtjefën's dance she hadn't yet known.

Lila and Shtjefën had just got married.

When she had gone back to Tirana, where she had been in college, the village of Rrnajë seemed so remote to Hana it made her head spin. She remembered wondering what she had been doing in that dump. She remembered calling to mind memories of cities and abstract poems written by foreigners in faraway lands. She remembered feeling like a stone at the bottom of a dark well. Her uncle was sick and bedridden; her aunt had just died. Hana had only the animals for company, and the poems she used to write now and then.

'Shall we go back?' Shtjefën asks Hana. 'I'm beat.'

Much later, when the Dibras are all asleep, Hana steps out onto the tiny kitchen balcony. She leaves the door open for a moment so the room where she'll be sleeping gets some air. Then she shuts the door, lights a cigarette and smokes it as calmly as she can, leaning on the balcony, trying to empty her mind. When she is able to do this, it is a particularly pleasurable exercise. She leaves her thoughts out and lets the silence in. It is a great sensation; she is full and empty at the same time. Her head lets air in, and the air acts as a kind of fan that refreshes the inside of her mind. She becomes aware of the pulse of her existence. It beats in her weak stomach, pauses for a while in her kidneys, which have never given her trouble. It is a simple, quiet journey. She feels like a rather undemanding tourist, lacking all curiosity. There is nothing she doesn't already know in there; nothing new to discover.

She runs her hand through her short, thick hair. Her shower that morning has softened it. Lila had urged her to use the conditioner after the shampoo and she had obeyed. She had even quipped something stupid like, 'You're already on a mission to civilize your cousin,' which had annoyed Lila. 'Don't start that crazy stuff,' Lila had answered. Hana had laughed.

Here you are. That's how they say it. Here you are. Her first American solitude. Her first night in this suburb, so like the films.

It feels like centuries since she left Rrnajë. She feels the shoulders and then the collar of her shirt. Lila's washer and dryer have already washed the smell of the mountains away.

She feels as though she is not herself; her name isn't Hana, her name isn't Mark. This feels like someone else's journey. She is watching the performance of a surreal dream.

So we go as we came,

goodbye, my brother sea.

There is no going back. She's been saying it for a year. If she leaves, there is no going back. At times, it sounds like a threat. At others, like a joke.

'Show them who you are, Mark Doda,' she had said out loud, on her own in the *kulla* that was slowly going to ruin.[4] 'Show them you have the balls.' The metaphor had made her laugh. But since then she had repeated it over and over. Show them who you are.

She is trying with all her strength. All she has to do now is work out how to go on.

One step at a time. First talk to Jonida, and see how it goes. Then talk to Lila, and see how it goes. She listens to the night; it's past three. There's no cock crowing. There are no mountains. Just night.

Back at Rrnajë, the Rrokajs' mad calf had started imitating the cock's crow every morning, at three on the dot, driving everyone crazy. Its translucent hide was dazzlingly white and it had two red patches on its face and one on its belly; it was the kind of animal that justified the expression 'good looking and stupid.' Soon after it was born, it had tried to suck milk from a goat. The village children laughed their hearts out. The goat kicked the calf away.

'What now?' Hana asks the night. She can see dawn coming reticently, hesitant on the horizon. She stubs out her second cigarette, decides she's had enough of these foolish thoughts and that now she can go to bed. She hears the balcony door open suddenly.

'You're not tired?' Shtjefën asks her. 'I'm off to work soon. So if you go to bed now, I'll be disturbing you for the next half hour before I leave.'

'No problem,' Hana whispers. 'I can sleep through anything.'

Shtjefën makes room on the balcony for Hana to go back in. He goes towards the bathroom. Hana closes the kitchen door, takes her pants and shirt off quickly and puts her light flannel pajamas on. She doesn't have time to fold her clothes; she thinks Shtjefën might come out of the bathroom before she's done. But he takes his time. She hears the shower running. She pulls the comforter up around her shoulders. Then she decides that tomorrow she'll talk straight to Lila about the division of labor in the house, and falls asleep.

The next day it's raining gently. This doesn't seem to pacify the hysterical traffic and the regular wail of fire sirens. The water lands on the sidewalk and trickles away in dirty brown rivulets. The flirtation between the trees and the fall goes on. The green leaves are compromised by touches of seasonal sunset red. Only the heat never lets up. It's relentless, obstinate, hard to bear.

Near the Dibras' apartment there's a supermarket, and there's a post office on the other side of the road. Downtown is a few minutes away by car.

'This location is great,' Lila tells Hana. 'When you need to go shopping or mail a letter, you can walk. For everything else in this country, you spend your life in the car.'

Lila blends in perfectly with all this, Hana thinks. She is clean and carefully groomed, and she's used eyeliner.

There are pancakes for breakfast. Lila announces that they're going to the mall to do some shopping, then starts firing questions at her incoherently. Hana listens.

She listens until Lila bursts out, 'What's got into you? Cat got your tongue?'

She shrugs. Her cousin points at the plate of pancakes, which has a transparent plastic lid on it.

'Try some. They're good,' Lila says. 'They're like our *petulla*.'

Hana tries them with maple syrup and melted cheese. They each drink two big cups of coffee.

'It's so nice to have you here,' Lila says with feeling. 'I have girlfriends here but there are some things about us I can't share with them. Now you're here I feel less alone.'

'But you have your family,' Hana objects. 'How can you feel alone?'

Lila empties her coffee cup.

'Your daughter is your daughter,' she answers. 'I'm the one should be listening to her problems, not the other way round . . . but maybe from your point of view that's hard to understand.'

On the wall there are photos: Jonida when she was little, Shtjefën and Lila on their wedding day with the whole clan proudly dressed for the occasion, a recent picture of Jonida during a volleyball game, Lila with a group of women. Hana wants to know where they were taken. Her cousin tells her about her nursing course and her graduation.

'That's as far as I got,' she says with a sigh. 'And I don't think I'll be able to go any further.'

'Why not?'

'Because I'd have to go back to school for years and I have a home to run and a daughter to take care of. I can't afford to pay for another course. It's too late now.'

Hana starts clearing the table and Lila lets her do it. They don't say another word until they leave the house and get into the car, a rusty old Toyota Corolla.

'I'm taking you to a great place now,' Lila announces.

They get onto a road that's called the 355 South, three lanes in both directions, more cars than she can imagine. Hana is overwhelmed with painful nostalgia for her old truck, which she sold to Farì, a mechanic she knew in Scutari. An old contraption from the days when Chinese cars were all there was, it wasn't even worth the 500 euros she got for it. She was amazed she had made any money at all.

'Tomorrow we'll go and register for your driver's license. You have to go through the whole works, eye screening, a knowledge test, and then your learner's permit. I'll take you out in Shtjefën's car, which is in good shape, unlike this old clunker. Remind me later on, I'll make a call.'

'There's no hurry.'

'Yes there is. Next week I'm going back to work and I won't be able to drive you.'

'There's no hurry.'

'Stop saying there's no hurry, will you?'

The mall is gigantic and sleek.

'You can even go to the movies here,' Lila explains. 'You can come in the morning, buy anything in the world, eat, catch a movie, and go home after a good day.'

'Is there a Barnes and Noble bookstore?' Hana asks, before they go inside.

'No, they don't have one here.'

'So it's not true you can buy *anything* here.'

Lila pushes her through the door.

'And how do you know about Barnes and Noble?'

Hana doesn't answer. She repositions her man's sports jacket over her shoulders. She likes wearing it without putting her arms in the sleeves. She looks broader in the chest that way, especially when her hands are in her pockets. She looks at the tips of her shoes. She's a 5½, and it was hard back in Albania to find men's shoes in her size. She always had to buy her underwear in the kids' department.

'We haven't come here just to stand around all day, eh!' Lila says, grabbing Hana by the arm. 'Come on, I need some caffeine.'

Hana turns around and holds her gaze.

'What the hell's got into *you*?' she asks. 'Of all the cousins in your family you could invite over here, you had to choose the weird one?'

'Is this something we have to solve here at the mall?' Lila quips.

'Why did you do this whole thing?'

'We've been talking about it for a year on the phone.'

'Answer me, now.'

Lila's profile is suspended between weariness and exaltation.

She doesn't want to talk, Hana realizes. All Lila wants to do is drag her into the depths of the mall and take her around the wonderland she thinks will help her to help Hana. Indeed, Lila doesn't open her mouth. She pulls her towards a café with little tables, where they take a seat. Lila goes and orders two espressos and comes back with a tray.

'You were not a happy man, Hana. That's all.'

'That's not true.'

'Ok, then, you tell me why you came.'

Hana looks out at the people carrying shopping bags of every shape and size, kids holding hands in a circle, two oversized women with their belly buttons showing. She can't believe it.

'You were not a happy man and you know it, just like you know this is coffee we're drinking. It's Italian, and delicious. And anyway, let's stop talking in this tragic way. I want to have fun today and be lighthearted. I want to enjoy you as you are now, in your last few hours as a man.'

Hana drinks her coffee in silence. The glass dome of the lobby lets in an uncertain sunlight that's trying to get past the clouds. Americans use weird words. A shopping center is a *mall*. In Albanian, *mall* doesn't squeeze money out of you, you carry *mall* around with you, you rock it gently in your arms. *Mall* is homesickness that consumes you, like *saudades*.

'Now I'm going to show you a store where we can buy some of the things you need,' Lila says, once again on her mission. 'In the next few days we're going to have to think about what to do with your hair.'

They walk into a huge store. Young assistants. Shrill voices. Dazzling smiles. Belly buttons of all kinds on show. Lila points out the fitting rooms, but then drops her arm. Her eyes betray her confusion. Which changing room? The men's one, with women's clothing? Hana looks at her, amused.

'This whole belly button thing,' she says, ignoring Lila's perplexity. 'It's not always such a good thing.'

'You and I have more serious things to think about!' Lila is getting nervous. 'Why didn't I think of it before?'

Hana doesn't want to try anything on. She's only there because she doesn't want to go against Lila's wishes.

'You can't go around like this,' her cousin says.

'I'll go around just as I've been going around up to now,' she mutters. 'Who's looking anyway?'

'I wanted to start doing something useful. Time shouldn't be wasted,' Lila answers.

'We're not wasting time. We're together, and that's what counts.'

'Have you taken a look at yourself in the mirror, Hana?'

'No, I never look.'

'There, you see?'

'What do you mean?'

'I'm sorry, I didn't want to hurt your feelings.'

'You haven't.'

'I'm useless at this.'

•

There was no need for mirrors in Rrnajë. Hana would leave the house and the first person she greeted on her path would be her mirror. *Tungjatë*, Mark. That was it. She had men's clothes and a flask of raki in her pocket, and these had also been her mirrors. She had needed nothing else. Up there in the mountains, time and place had been equal partners.

It is nobody's fault if at this precise moment she's so far away from there. She grabs her cousin by the arm and coaxes her up. They wander around the mall with no particular aim. It feels weird for Hana to spend time this way. She's never done it before.

'*Tungjatë*, Mark, *bre burrë, a je?*'

'I'm sorry for all this, Hana,' her old uncle Gjergj Doda had said.

'Don't say that, Uncle. It's not your fault.'

'Let me die. I'm tired. What is there for me to live for?'

'You can live for me, you're like my father.'

'A father marries off his daughter, he doesn't hang round her neck.'

'You're not hanging round my neck, Uncle Gjergj. You'll get better. I'll bring you your medication.'

'You know there's no cure. Hana, why sacrifice

yourself? You have to get married. You should be the sunshine in a house full of children.'

Hana hadn't said anything. Her uncle had hardly been able to breathe, there wasn't a blade of grass for the animals to eat, and she, at nineteen, had Walt Whitman's poems in her unopened suitcase. She wanted to get back to that book, but her uncle was there in front of her, more dead than alive. She was the only girl in the village enrolled in college. She hadn't wanted children, all she had wanted was books. But in the mountains you couldn't say these things if you were born a girl.

'May God help us, Hana, my little girl.'

'Amen, Uncle Gjergj.'

Her eyes are suddenly welling up and she doesn't try to hide it. The tears run down and tickle her lips. She licks them and tastes her homesickness. A boy is running into a shop called American Eagle and a young mother is running after him. 'Eddy, where are you going?' and then more words she can't understand. The way black people talk is hard for her to follow. More tears. She shuts her eyes, her jaw is trembling and she feels pain in the pit of her stomach.

'Hana, what's wrong?' Lila is shaking her, alarmed. 'What is it?'

'Nothing. I'm ok.'

'How can you say you're ok? You're crying.'

'I'm fine, Lila.'

'Why are you crying then?'

'I don't know. I feel like crying and so I cry.'

'You must be really sad.'

'Not even a bit.'

'Tell me the truth.'

'That is the truth.'

'Don't drive me crazy, tell me what's wrong with you.'

'Leave me alone, will you?'

Two Asian girls are following the scene without paying much attention, staring at Hana with their thoughts elsewhere. They speak to each other fast in a language full of vocal spikes. Hana tries to control her tears.

'I'm starting to get worried,' Lila says.

Hana moves closer to her.

'You don't have to worry. This is my battle, not yours.'

'I want to help you. I want you to be a normal woman as soon as possible.'

'You're ambitious, cousin. Ambitious and impatient.'

'That was the deal.'

'There's no hurry,' she mumbles. 'It's my soul more than anything, and I can't hurry my soul.'

'You're thirty-four,' Lila says. 'That's no joke.'

'It's not even half of my life.'

'You spent fourteen years as a man.'

'They're not lost.'

'If you go on thinking about it, you'll end up an old woman,' Lila says disapprovingly.

Hana strokes her hair. The precipitous voices behind her fade away. Turning around, she sees the two Asian girls have left. She turns back to Lila and hugs her, holding her tight. The two girls are replaced by a slim black woman with dreadlocks. Her tight dress is bright orange with pale-green embroidery round her ample cleavage. She looks beautiful, a goddess. Hana, wrapped in Lila's embrace, observes her. When they let go they both feel better. The woman in the orange dress allows her goddess aura to melt away as she pulls a CD player with earphones like Jonida's out of her bag. She fixes these in her ears and starts moving to the beat.

'What about another coffee?' Hana suggests. 'Then you can take me to that bookstore, Barnes and Noble. A guy on the plane told me about it. O'Connor, the journalist. Remember? I have to buy a dictionary.'

'I'll take you to the bookstore if we at least buy you some underwear first.'

'That's blackmail.'

'That's exactly what it is.'

Hana laughs, but Lila is serious.

'You don't have to try the underwear on. I'll just get some socks, underpants and something to go under your jacket – here they call them "tank tops." Ok?'

Hana shrugs. Lila gets up and sets off on a mission. She comes back with two bags of stuff.

'Now you won't have to worry about anything for a while,' Lila says as she settles back into her chair with an expression of victory on her face that Hana doesn't understand. It must be a woman thing, she thinks.

'Can we go to the bookstore now?'

'Tell me,' Lila insists in a tone that leaves no room for maneuver, 'what about bras? Have you ever used one?'

'No.'

'Do you have any idea of your size?'

'No.'

'But your breasts are small, right?'

'So it seems.'

'Does every little thing have to be such a problem? Soon Jonida'll be back from school. We've been here all morning and look what we've got to show for it – a few pairs of panties and not much else.' Lila opens the bags as if to prove her point.

'My small breasts have helped me not to stoop.'

'I get it.'

'No, you don't get a thing.'

'You may be right.'

'I love you, Lila.'

'Well, you tell me when you're ready then. I thought what you looked like on the outside would help you a little bit on the inside, but maybe I'm wrong.'

'You're wrong.'

'I thought that if you saw yourself from the outside . . . '

'I love you, Lila.'

'Ok, ok, I love you too.'

'I haven't said those words to any living soul since Uncle Gjergj died. It's hard not to be able to tell anyone you love them for so long. As for everything else, let's take it easy,' Hana begs. 'There's no hurry.'

'The thing is, you look like a guy trying to act effeminate,' Lila says, as if this were the last card in her hand. 'Your voice is odd, your face is rough. No one will give you a job if you look weird. People don't want problems around here; all they want is employees who are as normal as possible. You have to understand.'

'I'll tell them I'm a woman with a difference.'

'It's not so easy.'

'I can't go so fast, trust me.'

'Why not? You've had a whole year to think about it.'

'If I hurry, I feel terrible.'

She doesn't know a thing about the road they're on, but she stares at the road signs anyway. Lila turns the car radio on. Jazz. Hana looks out of the window. She then tries to memorize the junctions as they pass them on the 355. 'Is this normal life?' she wonders. She's been wondering for years what it would be like. The music is beautiful. She knows nothing about music but she knows she likes this.

Soon she'll be driving too; she just has to be patient a while and she'll have her own rusty old car. She has the money. She's saved up everything she earned taking wood down from the mountain to the town. She can't wait for the day she has her own car. She wants to tell Lila but she doesn't know how. Because I'm an outsider, Hana thinks. Just because I'm a cousin it doesn't mean she knows me. It just means I'm a cousin.

'Remember, Barnes and Noble is at the junction of Rockville Pike and Hubbard . . . Look at this, will you? I can't believe I have to take a hillbilly to a bookstore when she's only been in town for three days.'

Lila parks the car. On the left there's a café, on the right a homeware store. Hana is trying to memorize everything.

'Listen, Hana. Do you mind if I don't go in there with you? I don't know what to do in a bookstore.'

Hana says that's fine.

They split up and Hana goes in to explore. She looks around. Nobody seems to be paying any attention to her. She tries to relax but it's no good. To the right there are the counters where people are in line to pay. In front of her there's a huge table with new books on offer. Right behind her, the escalators.

She is frozen cold. It could be the air conditioning; she's not used to it. There are lots of people sitting in armchairs and reading near the store window. She hides among the shelves. Some readers are sitting on the floor and Hana decides to copy them. She dives into a narrow corridor between two bookshelves. The carpet is brown; her shoes are ridiculous. There are dictionaries all around her now. You're ridiculous, she tells herself. You're scared, you're still scared, but no one's looking at you. To her left there's a young woman, a student maybe, balancing a pile of books in her arms. She's wearing a pair of really nice glasses. She's dressed a bit like Jonida, only more sophisticated.

'Do you need any help?' she asks, after a moment.

'I need an English dictionary.'

'You've just arrived, right?'

'How do you know?'

The girl smiles. Her hair is thick and black. She's holding a pen, her nails are long and manicured, varnished silver.

'Five years ago I was going through the same thing. I was terrified, and I could hardly speak a word of English. The first thing I bought was a dictionary . . . They're right behind you,' she says. 'You're leaning on them.'

Hana turns around and sees them. She strokes them for what feels like a long time.

'Have you found anything?' Lila asks, tapping her on the shoulder.

'I'll get this. There's forty percent off. What do you think?'

'I don't know a thing about it, sweetie. Ask me about fabric, washing powder, drugs, how to make a bit of extra money on the side to get to the end of the month, anything, but leave books out of it. You don't think you're going to get a job here in America using books, do you?'

'I'll be a construction worker, don't worry.'

'They don't take women in the construction business.'

Lila checks her watch. They step onto the escalator. Hana steadies herself.

'I could be a taxi driver,' she says, gathering courage. 'There are women taxi drivers, right?'

Lila is tense. She looks at Hana, trying not to show it, and then reaches out to her, resting her arm on her shoulder. There's not much left of the pretty girl she once was. Back in the mountains there had been plenty of young men secretly in love with Lila. She is different now. She's got a frenetic look in her eyes. She's a bit homesick, which she tries to hide. And she's got enough love for her daughter to nourish the whole world.

On their way home, Hana is filled with a sudden euphoria. This is the third time she's taken this road – the 355, or Rockville Pike – and she feels as though she's known it for a long time. The rest won't be that difficult. All she has to do is talk to Jonida, explain things. All she has to do is turn into a woman, for real. All she has to do is learn the language. All she has to do is get a job and a room of her own. All she has to do is be normal. All she has to do is forget.

Forget.

Solitude; the death of glory in the mountains; her poems that would never become books; her last memory of her parents fixed forever on a winter's day.

'Where are you going to talk to Jonida?' Lila asks her.

'In the park we went to yesterday.'

'You don't want me to come with you, do you?'

Hana stares ahead.

'I want to be alone with her. Let's see if I can still spin a good tale.'

The park is almost empty. A couple in identical jogging pants runs by. A man jogs past them, pushing a gigantic three-wheeled stroller. Hana says it is four o'clock in the afternoon, just to say something. A family of ducks is standing in the middle of the lawn. The road behind the park is called College Parkway. It has taken Jonida and Hana ten minutes to reach this point.

They sit on a bench.

'So, Uncle Mark,' Jonida kicks off, a flicker of fear in her eyes. She crosses her long legs and her high ponytail catches in the wind. 'I've been thinking all day about what you're going to say, about all those things my parents hide from me, but I've guessed anyway, though I haven't said a thing to them.'

Hana gets her cigarettes out, but Jonida grabs them.

'They're bad for you.'

'What have you guessed?'

'We're here because *you* have to explain things to *me*, right?'

'I want to smoke.'

'It's bad for you.'

'I've smoked for fourteen years. One more cigarette isn't going to kill me.'

'Promise you'll stop soon?'

'Look, I'm not your father, ok?'

Jonida smiles for the first time and takes out one cigarette for Hana, then puts the pack away in her own pocket.

'So who are you in real life, Uncle Mark?'

'I'm your auntie, your mother's first cousin.'

Embarrassed giggles. Jonida suddenly uncrosses her legs and jumps up, facing Hana without actually looking at her. She looks beyond her, staring at the road.

'I know you're gay,' she says in an intimate tone of voice. 'That much is pretty obvious. But – '

'Wait a minute,' Hana interrupts her. 'Me, gay?'

'What's the problem then? Why is everything all hush-hush around you? You're homosexual. That's what I thought the moment I saw you.'

Hana bursts into laughter, but the smoke chokes her. She's laughing and coughing at the same time. She gets up too and they start walking. Jonida acts like she knows everything.

'You haven't done the operation yet, right? I mean, sexually, you're still a man?'

Hana hides behind her laughter.

'No,' she says finally, 'I'm not a man. And I'm not gay. Not even a little bit. I'm a woman. I've been a girl since the day I was born.'

Jonida slumps down on the grass. She's managed to find a spot where the newly cut grass doesn't prick her legs. Hana sits down next to her and puts out the cigarette she still hasn't finished.

'I'm not gay and I'm not lesbian,' she repeats. 'I know I look strange, a kind of hybrid, but I am a woman.'

'Where are your boobs then?'

'Here. Not very big ones, but I wear baggy shirts, as you can see.'

Jonida is silent. Hana gives her time to digest the information.

'Now I don't understand a thing. Starting with why you dress and act like a man. And how you managed to pass as a man, even though you were weird.'

'It's a long story,' Hana murmurs.

It is such a long story. She's already tired. To their right, a group of kids heads towards the big field where there's an oval of well-trodden earth.

'They're going to play baseball,' Jonida explains. 'Last year I was on the softball team but it was so boring I left. Now I play volleyball.'

Some clumsy kid hits his leg with the bat instead of hitting the ball. The coach makes him lie down. They all huddle around him.

'What do you know about the mountains, Jonida?'

Her niece thinks for a minute and then answers, pronouncing every word carefully. She knows that the mountains are really poor, that they're always shooting each other, that there are blood vendettas and family feuds. Her parents don't talk about it much. Lila says they're American now and should live in the here and now. She also knows that a boy from Montenegro in eighth grade at school speaks Albanian, not Serbo-Croat, which means there are Albanians in Montenegro, but not that many. She knows she'd like to go there some day, to see it with her own eyes. She'd like to engage with her country, some day.

'Maybe my story's not as complicated as it seems,' Hana says.

Her parents had both died in a bus accident while they were on their way to a wedding in the city. Those dirt roads were made for animals, not for trucks. Hana had been orphaned at the age of ten.

'Wait a minute,' Jonida says. 'You're going too fast, you're making it too . . . ' She leaves the sentence hanging in the air. That's how she takes after her father: her sentences made of air, hanging on invisible hooks. 'What's the death of your parents got to do with you deciding to be a man?'

Hana scratches her forehead.

'It's not that hard to be a man, you know?' she says. 'I swore never to get married. It's a tradition that exists only in the north of the country. Let me explain: when there are no boys in a family, one of the girls swears to behave like a man and to remain a man for the rest of her life. From that moment on, she has to play all the roles and take over all the tasks of a man. That's why I became the son my uncle never had. Uncle Gjergj was my father's brother; he took me in and brought me up after my parents died.'

'I don't get it.'

'I just gave you the basics.'

'I don't get it. Why doesn't the girl just do the men's stuff without having to turn into a man? Why can't she just do what she wants?'

Jonida's voice sounds alarmed. Hana feels guilty. She takes a deep breath and closes her eyes.

'So? Why can't she?' Jonida urges her on, realizing that her aunt is troubled by the question.

'Only a man can be the head of a family. Men are free to go where they like, to give orders, buy land, defend themselves, attack if need be, kill, or order someone else to be killed. Men get freedom and glory along with their duties. Women are left with obedience. And the girl I once was had a problem with obedience. That just about sums it up.'

She says this looking Jonida straight in the eyes, her words like sharp pins, accusing. But it's no good. Her niece can't be blamed for anything, except maybe having made her bring forth this perverse fairytale.

'I was a girl until I was nineteen,' Hana goes on. 'Uncle Gjergj and Aunt Katrina loved me.'

Jonida pulls Hana's cigarettes out of her pocket and hands one to her aunt.

'Then Uncle Gjergj got cancer. I had to go to the city to get his drugs once a month. I couldn't go if I was a woman. It was a matter of honor, morality, a woman's inviolability, and so on. I can't explain everything now.' Hana sucks on her cigarette. 'So I just started dressing like a man. Then Uncle Gjergj died, and here I am.'

Jonida fiddles with a button, plays around with the cigarette pack, rests her arm on Hana's shoulder, but she can't get comfortable. She gets up and then kneels down in front of her.

'Why couldn't you go back to being a woman after he died?'

'There's no going back.'

'Why not?'

'Just because. It's the law; it's tradition.'

'And if you do, what happens?'

'You don't do it, and that's that. If you break your oath they can kill you. Anyway, it has never happened. A sworn virgin has never broken her oath.'

'Did you like guys when you were a girl?'

Hana smiles, tired to the bone.

'Albania in those days was not like America now. We lived in the mountains. Things were different.'

'But did you like guys or didn't you?'

Hana repeats that up in the north things were different. They don't say anything for a while, eyes fixed on the baseball players. Then Jonida asks Hana what she should call her from now on.

'Just use my name. Forget the Auntie stuff. Call me Hana.'

'Mom's not going to like it.'

'I'll deal with Mom.'

'Right, cool.'

'Can we go home now?'

'You haven't told me everything yet.'

'It would take a lifetime to tell you everything, Jonida.'

'Well, that's exactly what we have: our whole lives.'

1986

'Thank God you're here,' Uncle Gjergj says. 'You made it with all this snow.'

The electricity is down. The snowstorm has stolen the light from all the houses in Rrnajë and the rest of the region. The power lines sag under the weight of the snow. Adults sink to their waists in the freezing mantle, children to over their heads. There isn't a living soul outside. Just silent snow falling, accompanied here and there by the distant ringing of a bell tied to the neck of some lost goat.

The hurricane lamp casts Uncle Gjergj's shadow onto the stone wall of the *kulla*.

'Welcome home, dear daughter,' Aunt Katrina says. She is tall and wizened with age, her hair hidden behind a white headscarf. She looks like Lawrence of Arabia, without the desert, Hana thinks. She saw the film back in Tirana. Aunt Katrina looks like a female version of Peter O'Toole.

'Are you hungry, my love?' Katrina asks.

'No, thank you.'

'We'll be eating soon anyway.'

'That's fine. Can I give you a hand?'

'No, sweetie. Your uncle needs to talk to you. I'll get dinner ready.'

Katrina disappears into the darkness of the *kulla*. Uncle Gjergj is lying down, which is not like him. If it weren't dark she would see his pallid complexion. But she doesn't see it. He is strong and handsome. The wrinkles on his face are a carefully drawn map.

'Did you bump into anyone in the village on your way here?'

Hana shakes her head.

She had seen the sea before coming to the village. Blerta, her college roommate, had come north with her. She's from a little village by the sea, near Scutari. Hana slept at her house the night before catching the bus that would take her home. The sea had been rough. Giant waves had vented their multi-hued rage.

Hana slept really well at Blerta's house. Wild horses wandered along the deserted beach; the sheets smelled of sea salt.

'Stay one more day,' Blerta had pleaded. 'You love being by the sea.'

She couldn't. Something serious had happened at home. Her uncle had never called her in Tirana before. He wouldn't have called without good reason.

Hana left clutching a bag of sand.

'I'll wait for you,' Blerta told her. 'We'll go back to Tirana together in a week. Remember, we've got a seminar on Renaissance literature.'

'Sure, Blerta. *Tungjatë.*'

'So you're already talking like the mountain people?' Blerta teased.

Hana liked using the *tungjatjeta* goodbye. Hand on heart, solemn gaze, the fleeting touch of foreheads to seal the sacred nature of the farewell. *May your life grow longer!*

She glances at her almost-decent city clothes. In the shadow of the *kulla* they look all right.

'I'm sick,' Uncle Gjergj says. 'There's this thing in my throat. They say it's big. Sometimes it chokes me and I can't speak.'

'How long have you known?'

'Two months.'

'The other day I dreamed you had a mountain on your back and you were stooped over with the weight. The mountain was made of dry earth and when you moved it crumbled around you so you were walking in the middle of a cloud of yellow dust.'

Gjergj laughs, the hurricane lamp making his mouth look bigger.

'Sit down,' he says.

Hana obeys. Between her and her uncle there is an ancient wooden table. He struggles to sit up in bed. Now Hana can see his terrifyingly swollen neck and the effort he makes to move his jaws normally while he's talking. He wants to know how college is going and she tells him that in a few days she has an important seminar on Albanian Renaissance literature. Gjergj says he doesn't know what a seminar is and she explains.

'And what is the Renaissance?'

'It's the cultural rebirth of a nation after a long period of darkness. Here in Albania the Renaissance was later than in the rest of Europe, not until the end of the Ottoman occupation.'

'It sounds like a complicated story, dear daughter.'

Hana doesn't say anything. Gjergj is an intelligent man but he often pretends he's not. She had no problem convincing him to let her go away to college. There are no books in the *kulla*, except a well-hidden Bible and a history of Skanderbeg, the national hero. That's the sum total. But she has always thought he knows much more than he lets on.

'Are you happy down in the capital?'

'Yes, very.'

'Even with all that communist garbage they thrust down your throats?'

The word 'thrust' is not a common word in these

parts. Not for a shepherd. Not for a man who can only write his own name. Hana is pleased with this confirmation of her suspicions.

'I like it anyway, even with the garbage. More than up here.'

'Well . . . ' Pause. 'I'm sorry I called you.'

'What do the doctors say exactly?'

'The bread's ready,' Aunt Katrina announces softly.

Neither Hana nor Gjergj heard her come in. Hana doesn't move. The old lady sits down next to her. Katrina has a bad heart and is only alive by a miracle. She is the love of Gjergj's life. The way they treat each other is not typical around here. Their dialect gives them away as mountain folk, not their gestures.

'I've made the beans. If you don't eat now they'll get cold, my love.'

Hana takes her hand.

'Can you tell me what's really going on, Uncle Gjergj?'

'They say I don't have long to live. Even if I have surgery, they don't think they can save me. I had to tell you in person.'

'It can't be true.'

'They say I've been sick for a while, I just didn't know it. Now it's too late.'

'You can come with me to Tirana. The doctors down there will say something different. They're the best in the country.'

Her uncle shakes his head. Hana feels a quiver in her stomach but she can't cry. She has never cried in front of him; it would disappoint him. The mountain peals with thunder. The snow is tired of falling. The roof of the hut is weighed down by two centuries of life.

'Everything's getting cold,' Katrina complains.

'You're coming to Tirana, Uncle Gjergj.'

Dinner is delicious. The potatoes melt in her mouth, the beans taste smoky and the bread is heavy and irregular. In the city the bread is white; nothing like this. Nobody says a word. Katrina envelops Hana in her gaze and they exchange glances only women can share. Life had deprived Katrina of children but given her a man who loved and treated her well. She suffocates Hana with her attentions: offers her a piece of roast onion, fills her bowl with beans again.

'You're still not full,' she says at the end of the meal.

'Oh yes I am. I've eaten a lot.'

'You've turned into a city girl, Hana,' Katrina says, smiling at her. 'You use different sounds, you speak like a schoolteacher. And your hair? What have you done to your hair? It's so beautiful.'

Gjergj looks at his wife surreptitiously.

'Tell me about the language of the English, dear daughter,' he commands.

'What can I say? It's a language that talks about beautiful places.'

Uncle Gjergj lights his pipe. He looks at the black patch on the wall to his left. He suddenly seems nervous.

'You think they're beautiful just because they're far away,' he says dryly. Then he shuts up.

In the days that follow, Hana's books are spread all over her room. There's a bed and an old wardrobe that hardly opens. Her clothes smell of wood and mold. No soap can wash away the smell.

One morning, Gjergj gets up and leaves the *kulla*. Neither Hana nor Katrina dares to stop him. He goes and smokes outside, in the snow. Sitting on a rough slab of wood in the middle of the courtyard, seen from behind, he looks like a sculpture. Then a cough assaults him and he defends himself as well as he can. His shoulders shudder until fatigue forces him to come back inside. He is deathly pale. Hana stares at him, her eyes wide.

Every six hours Katrina gives Gjergj the pills Hana doesn't even want to see. Her books are still open in her room. And she thinks that with this pain inside she's not going to go far. If you don't look pain straight in the face, it will take you over. It will inhabit you, a grubby black mass, a messy bundle. If you deal with it full on, on the other hand, there's a chance that it will leave you alone. She tries to take it on.

On the third day she puts on all the clothes she can

find and creeps out of the *kulla* unnoticed. She knows the path with her eyes shut. There's not much to see. Mist rises from the snow, obscuring her vision. After a while a runaway dog crashes into her legs. They are both scared. He's wagging his tail, staring at her. It's the Bardhajs' dog; he likes making love to sheep. He's the disgrace of his masters but the village kids' best friend. He won't bite. He licks her hand. Then they each go their own way.

When she enters the tiny village health center, there's nobody to be seen, but she can hear a child wailing in the other room. The doctor comes out, followed by the child's mother, followed by the only nurse, all smelling of talcum powder.

The mother is young, about Hana's age. She nods to her and leaves.

'Hi Hana,' the doctor says. 'Welcome home. How are you?'

'Good morning, Doctor.' Hana carefully avoids using the word 'comrade.'

'Did you just get here from Tirana?'

'No, I arrived three days ago.'

'Gjergj is very sick. He has cancer. I took him to Scutari myself, Hana. I'm really sorry.'

The doctor is in his thirties. He speaks a literary Albanian, his vowels open and his cadences perfect. He's in Rrnajë as a punishment. His family in the capital has a problem with the regime. It is rumored that some writer uncle of his had a few too many things to say.

'Uncle Gjergj has always enjoyed excellent health. He can't be *that* sick.'

'But he is.'

In a corner of the room there's a coffee pot boiling. Behind the doctor, the window is steamed up. On the wall to Hana's left is a portrait of the recently departed dictator, Enver Hoxha.

'How long has he got, Doctor?'

'Maybe four months. Maybe six, if he takes his drugs regularly.'

'He takes them.'

'He needs to take them without fail.'

'He'll take them.'

'Hana, you're not following me. The drugs are very expensive and the state does not provide them through the health system. They need to be picked up in town, in Scutari, once a month.'

'Don't you have a regular supply?'

He smiles, guardedly. So as not to show any dissatisfaction or discontent, Hana thinks. He opens his arms, as if in surrender. The white coat is thin from over-washing, almost see-through.

'I'm taking him to Tirana,' she says.

The doctor observes her. His gaze is desolate and his face anonymous, except for his curly hair, a bit too long in the front. That's prohibited by the canons of socialist aesthetics. He is sad for his own reasons, Hana decides. He's sad and lonely.

'A classmate of mine in Tirana is the daughter of a famous surgeon. Who knows? She might let me talk to her father and he might be able to help Uncle Gjergj.'

Hana gives the name of the potential savior. The doctor knows him; he worked for a while as his assistant before . . . He gestures something. Before being buried alive here, Hana guesses.

'How is my Tirana?' he whispers.

'Fine. Beautiful actually.'

'It's exciting,' she'd like to add, but she's not so stupid. The dictator died barely a year ago and the people in Tirana are waiting for a miracle to happen any minute now. At college, students spread the word quietly that the country may even open up to the West. Books that were prohibited now change hands furtively under the desks.

'You'll be going back soon, I imagine . . . ' He smiles, lost and vulnerable. He looks almost handsome. Suffering suits him.

There are some people who look good even when they're dead. She remembers her father's body. Her parents had been buried on a beautiful sunny day. Her father had not been good-looking in life, but he was when he was dead. They hadn't let her see her mother. Uncle Gjergj had said it was for the best. He had been right, she realized. *Nanë* had been really beautiful when she was alive.

'I'm not going back to Tirana without Uncle Gjergj,' Hana told the doctor. 'Will you help me take him?'

'Sure, I'll help you. I can go visit my parents, and I still have a few friends down there.' He plays around with a pen. 'Do you have any books with you, Hana?'

'Only in English. I've got Dickens' *Great Expectations* and the first volume of a history of Britain.'

'That would be great. Anything you've got. I'll give them back soon.'

'Ok.'

That is the end of their conversation. The nurse knocks on the door. Hana leaves. Halfway home, Hana bursts into tears. She looks up and keeps her eyes open wide. The snow finds its way into her eyelids. How do you settle your accounts with your soul when you die? It must be hard. Time to say goodbye to your body, time to weep your farewells, time to give up. The soul can't be hurried, it's not a magic trick.

She looks down again and sobs out loud. The snow-storm is a giant down comforter that suffocates her deep guttural sounds. She weeps for the doctor with the worn-out white coat, perhaps, or for the Bardhajs' dog that doesn't know how to love other dogs, only sheep, or again perhaps for the guy on her French course who had said in the canteen a few days before that she, Hana

Doda, was beautiful. She cries and cries and can't seem to stop.

The doctor arrives at the Dodas' *kulla* the next day. They have coffee together, then he examines Uncle Gjergj, measures his blood pressure, touches his swollen throat, and leaves him some cough syrup for when his cough chokes him. He sees Gjergj smoking his pipe and doesn't smoke one with him, but nor does he preach at him. Then he gets up. At the door, Hana hands him the two books.

Katrina and Hana watch him as he walks away. The doctor carries a rifle, like a true man of the mountains. If it weren't for his city gait you could almost take him for a local. The Party has given him a special license to carry a rifle because the wolves are particularly aggressive this year. One day they tried to get into the health center, they were so desperate for food. Mountain folk are no longer allowed to carry rifles, only guards and shepherds have permission. Gjergj Doda has a rifle because he's a shepherd.

The snow lets up for a while. The men from the electricity company come to raise the power lines, but they too sink into the snow and can't get on with their work. They give up and leave, their tools and some giant iron hooks deposited in the offices of the agricultural cooperative.

In the penumbra of the *kulla*, Uncle Gjergj is rasping. He can neither talk nor sleep. Hana keeps him company. Aunt Katrina sits beside him, stoking the fire in the copper grate.

'You should go, dear daughter,' Uncle Gjergj whispers. 'You need to get back to school.'

Hana looks at him. She would like to hug him but doesn't dare. She says that in two days, as soon as the road is cleared, she'll take him to Tirana.

'You're a stubborn one,' Uncle Gjergj says, his hands and chin trembling. He doesn't look at Hana for fear he'll begin to cry. Again she wants to hug him. But he falls asleep, hunched over, and Katrina lays a rough woolen blanket over his shoulders.

When they finally make it to Tirana it is already March and the weather down south is mild.

'We can try surgery,' a couple of doctors say, half-heartedly.

The public hospital is pulsing with activity. On the other side of the hospital wall there's a military academy. Hana, Katrina, and the patient sit on a green bench in the giant courtyard, waiting their turn for a second opinion. There's another group of doctors willing to examine Gjergj. Over the wall they hear an imperious voice whipping out orders, the clacking of heels, hands moving, the rhythmic clanging of metal. Weapons changing hands.

The village doctor is transformed. Shaved and well dressed, he has even put on some cologne.

'Strange things city people do,' Aunt Katrina murmurs. 'A man who wears perfume, *ku ku moj nanë*.'*

The doctor does everything he can. He talks to the doctors and nurses. He rushes from one place to another. He brings them *byrekë* pastries, he says you never know, there's always hope.

Hana went to the student-affairs office at the Liberal Arts Faculty and told them about her problem. She would have to miss a couple more days' classes; she just needed to take her father to see a few more doctors. Her parents were not familiar with Tirana and would not be able to cope without her.

'In your file it says your parents died when you were ten,' the secretary objected.

'The man who is sick raised me as his own daughter, so he is my father.'

'If you say so,' the woman muttered distrustfully.

Hana stared at her. She looked like a mole: brightly colored hair that failed to lighten her washed-out features, a rodent's jaw, foreign clothes. Rumor had it that her long-dead husband had been a diplomat. Hana had been warned by her classmates to watch out for this secretary. If she took against you it was bad news. She was a Party member and sometimes even raised her voice with Faculty members.

---

* A Gheg dialect exclamation expressing surprise, shame, perhaps a certain disapproval. Somewhat similar to 'what is the world coming to?'

'He's my father,' Hana insisted, as she left the office.

'Two days. You have two days' official absence and that's it,' the woman shouted after her.

The soldiers on the other side of the wall are marching. Aunt Katrina came down to the city wearing national dress. They're the best clothes she has. Decked out like this, she looks unreal.

Here in the city she seems less shy, she sits close to her husband and is not ashamed to touch him in public. Every now and then she lets out little shrieks of curiosity, breaking the silence. Uncle Gjergj is not unhappy to see his wife smiling.

'How do you not get lost here all alone, my love?' Katrina asks her over and over. 'All these people.'

Hana laughs. She holds Uncle Gjergj's hand tight. He looks so handsome today he could be in a Marubi portrait.[5] There are no signs of the disease on his face. Around his neck there is a red scarf, and he is wearing his dark-blue suit with a white shirt and a *qeleshe* on his head. He doesn't cough, he's not in pain, he doesn't ask any questions. He basks in the sun and lets Hana hold his hand.

Later, the doctors examine him, exchanging perplexed glances.

'We must operate,' they say. 'There's no time to waste.'

They take Hana into another room.

'Are you over eighteen?' one of them asks her.

'I'm a freshman here at the university. I just turned nineteen.'

'And you don't have any brothers or sisters?'

'No, it's just me.'

'What's your name?'

'Hana.'

'Listen, Hëna – '

'It's Hana, not Hëna.'

She loved her name. She loved the soft sound of the 'a' in the middle. Here in the south the vowel was more closed: Hëna.

'Hana sunshine,' her mother used to call her. She remembered her mother years back, when Hana was a little girl. She used to sing. If her mother hadn't been born in the mountains she would have been a singer.

Hana sunshine.

'You need to make a decision, young lady,' persisted the doctor who seemed to be the most senior. 'The sooner we perform surgery on your uncle, the better.'

'He's my father. Is there hope, Comrade Doctor?'

'We don't know yet.'

'Will he be in a lot of pain?'

'He'll be in more if he doesn't have the operation.'

'But there is hope; there must be hope!'

The doctors look at each other.

'There are no guarantees. But we'll do what we can. If we manage to remove the whole tumor he could make it.'

'Did you tell him there was a chance? The doctors in Scutari said there was no hope, and now he's convinced it's true.'

'Up there they don't know how to perform such a delicate operation.'

'What are our chances, Comrade Doctor?'

'Maybe thirty percent. Even if we can't eradicate the tumor, he'll still live longer.'

'How much longer?'

'Up to a year, maybe. Or more. Or less. Go and talk to your uncle. He doesn't want the surgery. You have to persuade him.'

'He's my father. I told you, he's my father.'

The hotel Hana has found for Gjergj and Katrina is modest but clean. The restaurant only serves rice and spinach.

'I thought it was only us up in the north who were poor,' Uncle Gjergj comments. 'But it looks like people in the city are not doing much better.'

He eats with gusto, even though it's painful to swallow. The waiter's uniform is crumpled. He doesn't show them much respect because he's heard their northern accents, but none of them minds. Katrina can't accept the fact that somebody is serving her at the table.

'Relax, Auntie, this is what they do here. It's a restaurant.'

'I'm so ashamed. Sitting here and being served by a man! What is the world coming to?'

'But he's a waiter. That is what he's paid to do.'

Their room is on the third floor. Hana is going to the college dorm for the night. In the morning she'll get up early so none of her roommates can ask her any questions.

As soon as they get to their room, Katrina falls asleep. Her heart has not behaved very well today. Before leaving the hospital, the village doctor gave her some pills.

Hana and Gjergj stand out on the narrow balcony. He smokes. Down on the street, people are taking their traditional evening stroll; nobody wants to go home.

'Why do you want to make me have this surgery, dear daughter?' Uncle Gjergj asks. 'You know there's no point.'

'The doctors say there's hope.'

'They're just experimenting on me, Hana. You're an adult now. You'll soon be a woman who knows about life. I've had my share in this lifetime. What's the point in my hanging on any longer?'

This must be the tenth time they've talked it over. His strength is leaving him. She can hear it in his voice, she can feel it in his hunched shoulders, however much effort he puts into standing up straight.

'Do it for me, Uncle Gjergj. Let them do the surgery for me.'

'I *am* doing all this for you. I don't want to make you or Katrina suffer.'

'What I'm saying is I want you to give it a try. Maybe the doctors will open you up and find it's not as serious as they're all saying it is.'

'I feel there's nothing to be done, Hana.'

'I beg you,' she says, melting into tears. 'Have the surgery. I've never begged you before.'

Gjergj says nothing for a long time.

'Just let me go,' he pleads, in the end.

Under the balcony a military truck goes by. The soldiers are sitting in two silent rows. The streetlights tint their faces sepia.

'What about Auntie? Don't you care about her?' Hana says, trying one last tack.

'Of course I care about her. We have talked, Katrina and I.'

'And?'

'She wants me to have the surgery too.'

'You see? How can you give up? You've never balked at anything.'

'What do you know, little girl?' Gjergj mumbles, his smile twisted. 'I certainly have! Many a time . . . but there are so many things you don't know. Our mountains under the communists . . . I'm not the man you think I am.'

What she's saying is heartless, she thinks. What *they* are saying, what she's asking him to do, this whole sea of words, it's all heartless.

'Just do it for me,' she tries one last time. 'I'm begging you on my knees. You've had a bullet stuck in your body for forty years and you've never complained. What's a scalpel to you?'

Hana can't stop crying. Her chin touches her neck and the tears drip down onto her dress.

It's not a heart, I say, it's a sandal of buffalo leather, it tramps and tramps, it never falls apart but treads the stony paths.[6]

'Fine,' Gjergj says. 'I'll do it. Now get out, before I change my mind.'

At that hour there are no buses, just the whirring of bicycle pedals: pairs of phantom wheels and the pale luminescence of the handlebars. The darkness hides the cyclists.

The dorm supervisor looks at her disapprovingly.

'Didn't they teach you how to behave?' he complains. 'What's a girl like you doing out alone at this time of night?'

Gjergj Doda goes in for surgery two days later. The doctors say it has gone well.

'Better than we hoped,' the village doctor, who had to go back to Rrnajë that day, pronounces. 'I'll come and pick Gjergj up when they discharge him. I'll get an ambulance. He'll be in the hospital here for at least two weeks.'

Hana notices that the village doctor wears the expression of a prisoner condemned to death. She'd like to ask him if he has a girlfriend in Tirana; what he misses most – the movies, or restaurants where they serve rice and spinach; what foreign books he reads in secret.

While he is talking to her, he observes her intensely.

She focuses on some graffiti painted on a broken wall. There are two letters missing: IN ONE HAND A ICKAXE, IN THE OTHER A RI LE.

She adores Tirana. She never thought she'd be able to love asphalt in the bottom of a valley. So she understands the doctor's desolation.

She has also realized that she does not pass unobserved in the school corridors. Her silence strikes people. Especially the boys, who try everything to get her to talk. Hana does talk to them, and their discussions tire her. She has got used to them; sometimes she'll even laugh.

'Why are you always sad?' a girl studying Turkish had asked her one day.

'I'm not sad. I'm waiting for something to happen that's worth talking about; anything else I just contemplate.'

'I was told you write poems.'

'Sometimes.'

'Can I read some of them?'

'No.'

The girl laughed

'You're weird.'

Hana gave a hint of a smile. The other girl had a head of hair the color of straw not yet burnt by the sun.

'My name is Neve and I'm studying Turkish literature. Do you know Nâzim Hikmet?'

'I've only read two of his poems, so I can't really say I know him.'

'Well, I'll give you some of his poems translated into Albanian. You'll really like him. I'll give you some that I had a go at translating myself.'

Hikmet sealed the friendship between the two girls. Hana fell deeply in love with the poet, and this might be one more reason why she loves Tirana. Here you could unearth new passions and meet new people, like Hikmet, like Neve, like the new words in her language, like all these writers who would never make it up to the mountains.

'Hana, focus now,' the doctor says. 'There's no more time. I have to go.'

'Thanks for everything.'

'Thank *you*, for the books, and for existing.'

Hana smiles shyly.

'Sometimes I feel really lonely up there. My friends are here in Tirana, and so . . . see you around. Will I see you in two weeks when I come back?'

Hana turns around and goes into the hospital. She's not ready for questions like that.

While they're waiting for Gjergj to recover from the surgery, Hana decides to surprise Aunt Katrina.

'I want to show you where I live,' she says, one day.

Gjergj is still wired up to the machines, but he smiles anyway.

'I'm borrowing her for a while, Uncle Gjergj.'

His woman-wife-friend-lover bends over and kisses him on the forehead. He can't stop her. He's immobilized. She kisses him again on the eyelids, right in front of Hana and a nurse. And then again. And again. Then Katrina and her niece leave the room arm in arm. Hana loves the way her aunt walks. When she was younger she used to try and walk like her but could never get it right. Her stride is vigorous and fast, despite her weak heart.

Hana guides Katrina onto a bus and sits her down. Her colorful outfit rings out like music among the dowdy passengers.

'How much is the bus ticket here?' her aunt asks her, intimidated and curious at the same time. 'What language is this?' she asks again, looking at the writing on the walls of the bus.

'It's French.'

'Why do they write on our buses in French?'

'The government bought them second-hand from France.'

'They had to go that far to find a bus?'

Hana sits next to her aunt and leans her head on her shoulder. Katrina kisses her hair. She is quiet for a while and then asks:

'Are the French communists?'

'No, what are you talking about? The French aren't communists.'

'Not even a little bit?'

'Maybe some people are, but the government is not.'

'So why did they sell buses to us?'

Katrina can't get enough of the city. She chats with the girls in the dorm, asking them where in Albania they are from. She looks out over the campus from the fourth-floor window. She pats Hana's bed and looks at herself in the mirror. 'Your aunt is so beautiful,' a girl from Durrës tells Hana. Katrina is embarrassed. Hana's roommates smile. One of them has brought a big onion *byrek* from home, and they share it out and wash it down with tap water. Katrina thanks everybody profusely and eats with gusto.

When Hana takes Katrina back to the hospital, visiting hours are over, but one of the nurses says she won't look if they slip into Gjergj's ward quietly.

He is sedated and fast asleep. Katrina gives him an adoring look, caresses the back of his dry hand, red and blue from the nurses' attempts to find a vein for the drip.

'One day, when you want to get married,' Katrina says to her niece, 'you'll find a good man like him.'

'If this man is so good, he won't want me.'

'Of course he will. With your schooling and your intelligence, and your foreign-looking face. It'll be love at first sight.'

'What do you mean by a foreign-looking face?'

'One that's beautiful and smooth like yours.'

'But I'm so short.'

'You're petite and beautifully built. Your breasts are perfect.'

'My breasts are tiny, Auntie. You can hardly see them.'

'You certainly can see them, if you don't walk all hunched up as if you're scared a man's going to look at you.'

Hana has never heard her talk like this.

'Well,' Katrina shrugs. 'We've never talked about these things, but we're in the city now so it's allowed, isn't it? I look at you, my love, I look at you a lot, but you never liked talking . . . '

Katrina strokes Hana's hair. Then she turns around and looks at her husband.

Hana's uncle and aunt leave Tirana on a beautiful spring morning. Gjergj is wearing his usual blue suit and manages to walk without any help. Next to him is the rolling drip stand.

Hana hugs both of them, hiding her eyes. She's already thinking about the distance that is about to separate them. She's happy they're going home. But she's sad too. She can't control her sobs. She's going to have to run back to the Faculty as soon as they're gone.

The village doctor promises her he'll get them to Rrnajë safe and sound, that he'll keep an eye on them even in his free time. 'There's not much to do up there, after all.' Hana thanks him.

'I'll call you when we get to the village, if you give me your number. You have a telephone in your dorm, right?'

She scribbles the number down for him, but she knows he'll never manage to catch her. Their supervisor is not the kind of guy who goes and looks for a student when there's a call. They say he works for the secret services, and nobody would dream of protesting or making an official complaint against him. Some even say he sends a report to the government every month about what the girls are doing and saying.

'I'll call you,' the doctor assures her.

An old, mud-encrusted bus drives past him, as slow and unsteady as a drunk camel.

'Do you have a boyfriend, Hana? Someone you like?'

From the back window of the bus, a boy sticks his tongue out at Hana and she smiles back.

'I have to go,' she says.

'Listen . . . '

'I'm not thinking about guys at the moment. I'm in the city. I have my books. That's already a lot for a girl from Rrnajë. You, of all people, should understand that.'

She turns around and leaves. Katrina's gaze brushes the back of her head. Hana can feel it. Gjergj, lying on the stretcher, stares at the roof of the ambulance. The nurse sitting beside him is thinking about the hellish journey she's about to make all the way to Scutari for some old man who's practically dead anyway.

Hana starts running; she doesn't want to take the bus. She's running as fast as she can to keep up with the ambulance, but then it turns down Kinostudio-Kombinat Road. Aunt Katrina is at the window, her fingers splayed, her eyes wide.

Hana blows her a kiss. The ambulance shifts up a gear and bumps along the road full of potholes.

This is the last time Hana sees Katrina, but she doesn't know that yet.

Katrina dies in the third week of June. Hana is ironing her blouse when a senior from her dorm comes into her room and hands her a piece of folded paper.

'It's a telegram. The dorm supervisor gave it to me . . . You're Hana Doda, right?'

Hana puts the iron down on the floor, takes the plug out, and hangs the blouse on the back of a chair. She'd like to drink something but the faucet is dry. She goes to the open window where the sun is beating down onto the half-drawn curtain. A couple of students are necking. The girl is quite ugly and not very bright, but her father is powerful. He works in the Central Committee of the Party, secretary or head of personnel or something. The girl is wearing foreign clothes, she can cut class whenever she wants, and she can neck in public without being considered loose. The guy is from the boondocks, in the south somewhere. He's really good-looking. Lots of girls are pining after him but he's ambitious and wants to stay in the city when he graduates, so he has chosen the right girl. She's really kissing him now. Hana looks at their hair: hers is shiny and soft because she has foreign shampoo; his is like felt because he uses laundry detergent.

She turns away from the window, sits down, unfolds the telegram.

AUNTIE DEAD STOP HEART ATTACK STOP FUNERAL DAY AFTER TOMORROW STOP

Her last exam is in three days. If she doesn't take it she won't be admitted into her sophomore year.

She throws a few things into a bag, runs out of the room and down the stairs to the ground floor where there is running water. She puts her mouth under the faucet and drinks at length. She wets her arms and pats water behind her neck. It's three in the afternoon, and no way is there a bus for the north at this time. No train either. She'll have to wait until tomorrow.

She is unable to leave even the next day. The train is broken and can't be fixed, they say. The passengers in the station are furious.

If they want, they can come back the next day, but 'there are no guarantees,' a fat railroad clerk announces, scratching his belly. His uniform is buttoned wrong, covered in stains, the collar worn thin. A herd of sheep makes its way through the crowd, indifferent to the human suffering around it. The sheep make do with the last of the grass between the railroad sleepers.

Hana is immobile. The crowd slowly disperses. A few older passengers just sit there with pages torn from the official Party newspaper, *The Voice of the People*, folded into hats on their heads.

After an hour or more she decides to walk to the central post office, where there are some public telephones. When she gets there she counts her change. She'll only be able to talk for a minute, or she won't have enough money for the train ticket the next day.

The secretary of the agricultural cooperative in Rrnajë says that nobody is in the health center. The doctor has gone to the Dodas' because Katrina has died.

'This is Hana. Hana Doda.'

'Ah, sorry. I didn't recognize your voice. I can hardly hear you. I'm sorry.' There are the sounds of others on the line.

Outside the phone box, there's a man with three children waiting his turn. He must be a baker; he's covered in flour. Two of the kids are gripping his legs, the other is perched on his shoulders.

Hana asks the secretary if she can go and call the doctor. She'll wait at the post office.

'Ok . . . They say your aunt didn't suffer, Hana. She was crocheting you a vest and that's how she died. Smiling. She seemed at peace, if that makes sense.'

Hana waits an hour and seven minutes before she is able to talk to the doctor. The heat is stifling. The hall of the post office reeks of feet and armpits.

'Hana. The doctor here.'

'I can't get there. It was her heart, wasn't it?'

'Her heart, yes. It's already a miracle that she lived so long. The funeral is tomorrow at noon.'

'I can't get there by then.'

'We can't do anything about it. It's hot here. The body . . . I'm sorry, Hana.'

'You're a doctor. Can't you invent something to keep her body cool?'

'Doctors don't work miracles, and there are no morgue facilities here. I'm sorry.'

For once her cursed mountains could have stayed cold.

'If the train leaves I'll get there tomorrow evening late. If it doesn't, then I don't know.'

Somebody at the other end of the line is grumbling and the doctor shouts, 'Just a minute, please. It's the Dodas' daughter.'

'I'll tell Gjergj you called,' he goes on, resuming his normal tone. 'He's doing well. He's getting his strength back. Now I have to leave the phone free. There's the Comrade Secretary of the Party here and he needs it.'

The doctor hangs up before she can say ok or thanks or anything. Hana rests her forehead on the graffiti scratched

in the wood of the phone box. Somebody has written: I'VE
NEVER MISSED YOU.

She arrives in Rrnajë when it is almost evening. The house
is empty; everybody has already left. The *shilte* are in a
mess on the floor.[7] Her uncle is sitting up. Hana bends
down and gives him a hug.

'It took so long, Uncle Gjergj. Forgive me. Nobody
was coming up today. I had to wait two hours in Scutari
before a truck going to Bogë came by.'

'The doctor sent you the telegram. He's been a great
help. You must be hungry.'

'A little.'

'The village women have brought food for a week.
Go eat something.'

'Ok.'

But Hana doesn't move. She stays where she is, staring
at the *kilim*. They don't say a word. Gjergj starts rolling
a cigarette, but then changes his mind and fills his pipe.

Hana jumps up and starts plumping up the cushions.
She opens the narrow window. There's still a trace of
sun in the color of the sky, a hint of yellow drowned
in blue.

'Up here it's too hot for June. What about down in
Tirana?'

'Even the dogs are sweating.'

Hana picks up her bag and drags it upstairs. Her room is in perfect order. Nobody has been in to take a nap during Katrina's vigil. Somebody, though, has laid an unfinished white cotton crocheted vest on the pillow. The crochet hook was threading a red border round the waist when it came to a stop. All that's missing are the buttons and a pocket. It would have been a beautiful vest with a red border. Almost city wear. Her girlfriends in Tirana would have envied it.

She sits on her bed without touching the vest. Uncle Gjergj is coughing downstairs. She lets him. When the silence wraps itself around the walls she decides to go down.

They sit curled up on the cushions. Hana has forgotten her hunger. He goes on smoking. She falls asleep.

Gjergj starts wheezing around dawn. He groans and rattles, and asks her to pass him a spray for his throat. The spray smells really strong; it's terrible. He is sweating and trembling. He finds it hard to breathe but doesn't want any help.

'Just go and check on Enver,' he manages to say to Hana. 'I don't know if he has eaten, poor creature.'

Hana leaves the room and goes to the animal pen in the courtyard where their goat and sheep live. The sheep is sleeping, the goat is not. As soon as he sees Hana he starts bleating.

'Hi Enver,' Hana says, stroking his beard. 'How're you doing?'

She looks around her. The hay is fresh, the water pail has been filled. Somebody has taken care of everything before leaving. The nearest neighbor's *kulla*, to the left, is ten minutes away. Nobody lives on the right, there's just the sharply rising mountain.

A woman who came to Katrina's funeral brought the traditional offerings of tobacco, sugar, and coffee. Maybe she cried, and then went to take care of the animals. It must have been Dille, Ndué Zega's wife. The two families help each other out, without making a show of it. The Zegas have a son who works in the Party as a member of the Citizens' Committee in Lezhë. He doesn't approve of the Dodas. They are a little too Catholic to be politically reliable.

The communists have always doubted Gjergj's faith in the regime, but they have never caught him out in any way. Gjergj Doda is canny. He has never expressed a point of view regarding the government. Better not to talk at all than to say something against them. He's a good peasant. He sticks to the communist rules, except for the name he has given his goat. He has secretly called him Enver, like the dear departed leader, but this small detail nobody knows about.

'See you later, Enver,' Hana says as she leaves the pen. 'I'll come by and visit tomorrow when I have more time.'

The next morning she goes on her own to the village cemetery. The sun is shining and the tractors from the agricultural cooperative are already plowing their way up and down the few tracts of amenable land. The rest is so steep it can only be farmed by hand.

Katrina's grave is easy to spot. There are fresh flowers stuck into jam jars and bottles.

She touches the freshly turned earth and quickly pulls her hand away. Then she touches it again, this time digging her fingers in and leaving them there.

'Thank you for my vest, Auntie,' she says out loud. The collar of her blouse is dripping with sweat. 'I'm sorry I didn't get here in time.'

She realizes that she should be in the exam room right now, in the auditorium next to the dean's office.

She sits down on the ground. Her knees are killing her. She pushes her other hand into the earth and bows her head until her chin touches her breasts.

She tries, but can't seem to make herself cry. Suddenly tears of anger that she doesn't feel like crying fill her eyes.

After an hour, she goes home.

Uncle Gjergj is hunched up, trying to keep the spasms of pain under control. He can hardly speak or move his arms.

'My whole body is hurting. Leave this house, Hana. Stop looking at me.'

In the daylight she can see the mess left by the mourners after the funeral. Aunt Katrina wouldn't have stood for it.

'But Uncle Gjergj . . . '

'Go away, I said. Get out of here. Did you leave your obedience in the city? Have you forgotten your manners?'

She leaves the room. She starts boiling a pan of water, in which she'll throw the ash from the fireplace. Aunt Katrina always saved it to use instead of soap when the shops in Rrnajë are out. She goes into the storeroom and looks for the aluminum pail full of ash. If you boil sheets in water and ash they come out white as snow.

She opens the upstairs windows wide. There are three big rooms under the gables. She would be coming out of her exam now. She would be admitted to the second year. She would be happy.

The day continues to be marked by the heat and the sounds of their animals. From the Dodas' *kulla* you can't see the village. Hana can start cleaning; she can take off her blouse and wear only a camisole without looking indecent. Nobody will see her.

Would Ben, her classmate in French, have finished his last exam? She likes the way he looks at her. She tries to focus on wiping the glass in the tiny window.

When she has finished cleaning the house it looks like new. Gjergj is still. The pain has let up for a while and he's finally gone to sleep. Hana is pleased with herself, with how she organized her day and how she managed to enjoy the sun upstairs while she cleaned and tidied things up. Her arms are pink, slightly sunburnt.

The girls in Tirana strip off in the park, as much as they can, as much as the laws imposed on them by men and communist morality allow. The girls in Tirana cut classes and go to the beach in Durrës. One day she'd like to go herself, but she doesn't have a bathing suit.

Goodbye, my brother sea.

The doctor arrives while she is cooking dinner.

'I'm here to give Gjergj his drugs, but since you're here I'll show you what to do,' he says.

Hana asks him to step outside where they can talk, as her uncle is sleeping.

'I'm sorry about Katrina,' he says. 'My condolences. And Gjergj is sick, Hana. The operation didn't help much.'

She says brusquely that she doesn't want to know and he answers that maybe she should listen to what he's saying because soon she'll be on her own and that's the truth. He hands her three boxes of medicine.

'I'm sorry, Doctor. I'm really confused right now.'

Silence.

'Do you remember, Hana? You were the first person I met here in Rrnajë, the day I arrived.'

She feels sorry for him.

'Yes, I remember. You smelled of aftershave. The whole village knew you were arriving that Tuesday.'

He clenches his jaw. She looks at his profile.

'I like you,' the doctor says. 'I'm getting to like you more and more. I thought it would blow over, but you've stayed in my mind.'

Hana turns away. The mountain is growing dark, preparing to be abandoned by the sun.

'How can you like someone like me?' she asks caustically. 'Don't you city people call us *malokë*?[8] Don't you always look down on us mountain people?'

He doesn't feel he can contradict her. He's honest enough to admit it to himself, at least, if not out loud. That's better than nothing, Hana thinks.

'What were you reading before coming up to Rrnajë?' he asks, trying to buy some time.

'*Death of a Traveling Salesman.*'

Hana puts her hands in her pants pockets. They are black, made of light flannel. She thinks they look quite good on her. She found them in a shop in Tirana, and the mother of a classmate of hers, a seamstress by trade, took them in a little. The doctor waits for her to say something and, when she doesn't, he asks if by any chance she has anything to say about what he has just said.

'You're a regular kind of guy; you must have had a lot of beautiful girls,' she snaps, without even looking at him, almost turning away from him. 'Why are you bothering with me? Or is it just because I'm around?'

'That's pretty mean,' the doctor protests.

Hana would like to rest her head on his chest to see what it feels like, to see what a man smells like close to.

'You've chosen a bad day to declare yourself.'

'I've been meaning to tell you for a while. And anyway I'm leaving in a few days.'

'Leaving?'

'They've transferred me . . . So?' he insists. 'Any answer?'

'Give me some time,' Hana says, amazed by her own words. 'I have to think about it. Don't get your hopes up though.'

The doctor says he doesn't understand. If she asks for more time it means there must be hope, otherwise there would be no point. She stops him and says that's the way it is, and that's that. The truth is she doesn't want to lose him. If she just said 'no' she would be burning her bridges, closing all the doors, letting the darkness in. This realization makes her feel terrible, because she's not attracted to him, not one bit.

'You must understand that I can't wait long,' he says. 'I've been transferred and I'm finally going to be closer to home.' Hana notices the stress he puts on the word 'finally.'

'So you're going back to Tirana?'

'I wish! No, I'm being sent to Kavajë. It's much closer to Tirana and much better than here.'

'So you're free,' she smiles bitterly. 'You're free.'

All at once he steps forward and kisses her on her forehead.

'Free from what, Hana?' he mutters, while she pulls away from him. 'Free from where? We're just like horses, going round and round in circles.'

They catch each other's eyes for the first time. He has nice eyes, she's never noticed before. She would like to tell him so, but senses she has missed her chance. Something in him shifts. The shared confidence about the concept of freedom has made him wary. He's under control. He's the doctor now.

'It's best not to talk about certain things, young lady,' he whispers, 'if you don't want to get into trouble.'

'Why? Aren't I already in trouble?'

'There's a lot worse, and you know it.'

'So now I'm "young lady," am I?'

Hana turns away and takes a few steps. Life is strange. There are some things she's never said before, never talked about, never thought she could say so freely. Now all this for some guy whom she doesn't really know or particularly like. But she's still sorry he's leaving.

'It's a strange life, Doctor.'

'Would you like to call me Artan finally?'

He comes dangerously close again. He's just behind Hana; his breath is hot and sad.

'Ok. It's a strange life, Artan, because I'm sorry you're leaving.'

'So . . .'

'There isn't any "so." I'm sorry, that's all.'

She turns her back to him, her eyes brimming with tears. She suddenly starts sobbing, her hands on her stomach.

'Go on, cry. Get it out of you.'

'I can't.'

'Just let yourself go, Hana.'

He hugs her. She lets him. She rests her head for the first time ever on the heart of a man. They stand there together for a while. Here's why it's such a good thing to have your house on the edge of the world: nobody can see you; nobody can betray you.

'If you will allow me,' he murmurs, 'I'll ask Gjergj for your hand. I know that in these parts there's no other way to have a relationship with a girl, so I'll ask him for your hand in marriage.'

She detaches herself brusquely.

'Who do you think you are? I don't love you and I don't know you, and anyway, who says I need a man?'

Her uncle has woken up and is thumping his stick against the wall to get her attention.

'I have to go in,' Hana says, cutting the conversation short.

The village is without a replacement doctor for a long time. The Ministry of Health doesn't have another man to sacrifice to the mountains. The only nurse decides to devote herself to sick children, leaving the adults to fend for themselves.

'Hana, my girl,' the nurse says one day. 'You need to go down to Scutari to pick up your uncle's drugs. I can't do everything, and anyway it's dangerous, a woman all alone . . . I'm married and my husband won't allow it.'

'They wouldn't give me the drugs, Comrade Nurse. They're imported.'

'I'll call the pharmacist in Scutari,' the nurse reassures her. 'I know him personally.'

The nurse is in her forties, but her expression makes her look older, almost ancient. She observes Hana with curiosity, her big eyes boring into her.

'What about you? Aren't you going back to Tirana?'

'I'll go say goodbye to a few friends and find out when I can retake the final exam that I missed.'

'I've never been to Tirana, I've only ever seen it on TV. Is it really that beautiful or do they make it look that way so that we mountain people envy them?'

Hana thinks about it.

'There are buildings and asphalt,' she says finally.

'And I suppose your shoes don't get muddy?'

'It depends.'

More silence. The nurse's curiosity goes into standby.

'I'm tired,' Hana says, and goes out without saying goodbye.

•

Gjergj tries to keep his pain under control, but when he has no energy left to fight it he turns nasty.

'Get out of here! Go away! I don't want you here!'

She obeys and takes refuge in her room with her books. She leafs through them, but the feelings she once had for them have turned into smoke that chokes her suddenly. She doesn't love them anymore, and she feels guilty.

One day she tells her uncle she has to go down to Scutari to get his drugs. He looks a little better this morning; his expression is lively and a vein is pulsing on the back of his hand. He shakes his head.

'I have to go,' Hana says. 'You only have three days' worth of medication here.'

He's still against it.

'I'll go tomorrow morning with one of the trucks carrying wood down to the city. I expect a driver will have room for me.'

He waves his arms in total disapproval.

'So tell me, what should we do?' Hana asks rudely. 'You tell me, since you know everything. Am I supposed to stay here and watch you suffering without doing anything to help?'

He looks daggers at her, tries to say something but lets out little more than a grunt.

'Yeah, I know, Uncle. I'm a woman and I shouldn't be talking like this. I should know my place.'

He grabs the stick that he keeps by his bed and thumps it on the table. His hand is so unsteady that the stick falls onto the worn-out *kilim*.

'I'm sorry,' she says, as soon as she gets over the shock. 'Forgive me . . . Will you forgive me?'

She hugs him. She curls up between his shoulder and his chin. Gjergj's heart is a drum that has lost its beat.

'You can't go alone, my little one,' he whispers in her ear. 'It's dangerous.'

'I'll try. Look, I know how to take care of myself.'

'There are wolves out there, my daughter. This place is full of wolves.'

There is a brief, transparent moment of silence. Then Hana decides to play along with her uncle.

'It's summer, Uncle Gjergj. The wolves aren't that hungry.'

She gives him a couple of pills that are supposed to help him sleep. Then she goes up to her room and stands by the window listening to the late afternoon: the dialogue between plants and animals, life twisting up and then stretching out. A year ago, Hana would have been moved by such beauty; now she is calmly detached. She feels grown-up and she likes it.

'You're Hana Doda,' she says to herself out loud. 'Hana Doda, daughter of Felicità.' Her mother's name had been Happiness. Aunt Katrina always said she had had a beautiful voice. Hana remembers her singing around the house. Why was she thinking of this now?

'Now I have another problem. See, *Nanë*? You've come along at the wrong time.'

Everything is wrong. Even this summer, that seems like a wonderful painting but isn't, if you look at it carefully. This summer looks more like a mediocre poem. Albanians write a lot of poetry, they're crazy about poems, but they're scared of telling stories. You need persistence to narrate a story, as well as discipline. Full sentences don't allow you to cheat or be lazy. Poetry does: it's more worldly-wise, more fleeting, more musical. Narration is for monks, inscribing manuscripts all day until they're hunchbacks.

'Don't you see, *Nanë*? I've got other things to think about. Go away!'

Hana waits until the memory of her mother fades. She can feel it shrinking fast, and then vanishing.

She feels lost.

She takes it out on her English dictionary with its blue, black, and yellow jacket. It's called Hornby. Mr Hornby thinks he's so great that he can teach you a language. She wonders whether the gentleman is still alive. Is he sad? Lonely? Ugly? She imagines him to be thin and bespectacled, not good-looking. With a pencil she scratches a picture of the imaginary Mr Hornby on the book jacket.

'Serves you right,' she says rancorously.

At the first light of dawn she sets off for Scutari and returns to Rrnajë late that night. Everything has gone well. She didn't meet any wolves, and she has the drugs. When Uncle Gjergj sees she is back he looks at her with infinite love.

The driver that had given her a ride into the city was in his fifties and had no desire to make conversation.

'So you're Doda's niece,' he had said at the start of the journey. 'I knew your dad. He was a good guy. How's Gjergj?'

'Sick.'

'So I heard, I'm sorry.'

That had been the end of their exchange. The truck had gone so slowly that if Hana had walked beside it she wouldn't have had to pick up her pace.

'I do this trip once a month,' the driver had said at the end of the journey. 'If you want I'll take you down every time. You know it's dangerous, don't you?'

Hana had nodded.

'Has Gjergj arranged a marriage for you? Have you been promised since birth?'

'No.'

'Be careful, girl. And give my best to your uncle.'

Gjergj's room smells stuffy. She changes his neck scarf, which is soaked with sweat. In the courtyard Enver is making a ruckus, bleating like crazy and kicking the door to his pen.

'You see, it wasn't so bad after all,' Hana whispers to the old man. 'The pharmacist was really kind and wrote down all the instructions for me.'

Gjergj gestures that he's thirsty. She brings him water.

'I have to feed the animals now, then I'm going to buy a little fresh cheese.'

Hana doesn't know how to make cheese yet. She'll have to learn. Aunt Katrina did everything; she can't do very much.

'You're a good girl,' Uncle Gjergj mutters. 'Such a good girl, you're my boy. You're like a son; the things you're doing are men's jobs. Going off alone and coming back in the middle of the night across the mountains. You need the courage of a man to do those things.'

Hana laughs out loud, pleased with the compliment.

'If you'd been born in the city you would have been a real ladies' man, Uncle Gjergj.'

'I am,' he answers. 'You have to go back to Tirana, get back to your studies. Have you forgotten?'

Hana answers that she can't leave him in this condition and he says yes you can, what else can happen to him?

'There's no discussion, Uncle Gjergj. I'm not leaving you alone.'

'It's an order, Hana. I'm not asking you. I'm ordering you to go.'

Their short argument takes a long time. Uncle Gjergj loses his thread and smiles. He seems to take stock of every phrase and delays looking at his interlocutor until he has decided to expel his words, one after the other, slowly. Hana has learned to adapt to his rhythm.

'Classes are over, Uncle Gjergj.'

'But they start again in September, right?'

'Why should I go back? I'm not going back to school, it's not worth it at this point . . . '

He starts moving, as if he wants to get up, and then looks at his stick but can't reach it.

'Ok. I'll go to Tirana,' she eventually concedes.

'Go to the student office and make all the necessary arrangements to enroll again in September.'

She sets off, leaving her uncle to the sporadic care of the village nurse. She gets a ride with the agronomist from the cooperative, who is taking a jeep down to the city for an important meeting. She gets a train from Scutari, which breaks down in Lezhë, so she has to wait for whatever ride she can find.

She gets to Tirana at nightfall. It is hot, the roads smell of melted asphalt. The center of the capital city is dark. In order to save what little power there is, they don't turn the streetlights on. She's happy to walk along the clean streets, wending her way to her dorm. It is almost empty, as most of the students are home for the summer vacation.

Hana has the room to herself. She goes to bed and sleeps soundly.

The next morning the Liberal Arts Faculty is deserted. The heat is overpowering. The bad-tempered secretary gives a highly acid, 'What do you want?'

'I've come to say that I'd like to do my last exam in August.'

'Who said you could?'

'I'm a student in this Faculty.'

'Who didn't take her exam and disappeared from the face of this earth without any justification.'

'My mother died, Comrade Secretary.'

'How many mothers have you got? One seems to die every year.'

Hana stares at her reflection in the glass pane of a cupboard. She thinks she looks quite pretty, in a blue and red checked shirt with two big pockets. She shifts her attention back to the secretary.

'My aunt, who became my mother after my parents died in a car accident many years ago, she died. And my uncle, her husband, is very sick with cancer. He's all I have left.'

The woman tries to look sorry, but fails. All she can do is tone down her sarcasm.

'You could have come and asked permission.'

'I didn't have time. I asked my classmates to do it.'

'That's not sufficient, young lady. The trouble with you mountain people is that you never learn to obey rules.'

Hana looks back at herself in the glass and adjusts her curly hair. She directs a faint smile at the perfumed hyena who, in the meantime, has improved the color of her hair-dye.

She is suddenly seized by the thought that she has to go to the sea. She leaves the office before the secretary can open her mouth again.

It is Friday.

The sea is majestic, polished and shimmering like a perfect dream. Nothing detracts from its immensity, neither the garbage rotting on the beach nor the ungainliness of the few bathing costumes on show.

She has found a quiet spot near Durrës. There are only two families with kids. She looks around, then closes her eyes and tries to empty her mind of thoughts. She only partly succeeds. Her demons are still there, but they are polite and almost harmless now. They smile at her.

The sand burns her feet. She has thrown her deformed shoes under a rock and tied her hair in a ponytail.

She steps into the water in her pants and shirt, with all the money she has in her pocket. She can't afford to have it stolen because it's her return fare to Tirana. The folded bill will enjoy a swim in the sea. The salt will fix the color of her black pants. The water will wash the smell of dung out of her shirt.

The salt is drying on her skin and the tightening sensation forces her back to the here and now. She'll be taking this salt home with her, for she has no change of clothes. They will dry off and she'll be fine. She'll be fine, she says. And she really is fine, for the three hours she's at the beach.

So we go as we came,
goodbye, my brother sea.

The next day she goes to the college library and returns all her borrowed books. It's nine in the morning and at that time there are only a couple of professors. The librarian is a man to be respected; his smile is reassuring and his manner affable. He asks Hana if she wants to take any other books out.

'No, this time I'm just returning them, thanks.' The man goes back to his work.

She spends an hour in the reading room, leafing through a volume of Emily Dickinson's poetry. There's no point taking notes; it's best to leave without saying goodbye. But she can't resist. She takes out a pencil and some paper and copies out a few poems.

The librarian looks over at her every now and then from his desk.

'You can take it if you want,' he says in the end.

'I live in the north and I can't return it on time. I can't come down specially.'

'You can keep it until the end of August.'

'I'm not coming in August,' Hana says, waiting for some kind of response. Go on, ask me something, she begs in silence. But the man doesn't ask her anything. He turns away, hunched, as he files the index cards in their file, writes something in a register, and forgets all about her.

'Have a good day,' Hana says, too softly to be heard, and leaves the library.

When she gets to the gate of the School of Philology she looks one last time at the edifice, built by the Italians during the Fascist occupation. Her clothes are starting to itch. The sun beats down even more fiercely than yesterday; sand and sweat make swirling lines like maps or flowers on her pants.

Hana starts walking fast towards the center, but just as she is past the Italian embassy gate a boy's voice calls her. She turns round. It's Ben, the classmate who studies French.

'That's the third time I called out your name,' he complains. 'Are you deaf or something? Hello? Hana?'

She's unsure whether to hold her hand out or not.

'Here she is! The girl who just disappears without any warning. How are you?'

'Fine.'

He says he's sorry about her aunt's death, the girls from the dorm told him. Hana tries to control her breathing; her heart is beating fast. She stares right into his eyes so that he can't see the effect he's having on her. Calm down. Stay still. It's just some guy trying to be nice. And you're such a mess in your crumpled pants.

He asks her where she's going. She says she's going home after returning her library books. She smiles. Ben says he is on his way to the Faculty. His hair would make a girl jealous, it's so glossy and healthy-looking. His eyes burn into you when you look at him. Their slant makes him both hard to grasp and insistent at the same time. It doesn't make sense, she thinks. He's just trying to be nice. Ben smiles.

'I've been looking for you,' he says. 'I've been waiting for you for a long time.'

If she really had to force herself to like a guy, given that it was the cool thing right now to be in love, Hana would choose Ben. That way she wouldn't seem so out of place. She would choose Ben – but it was only a silly thought.

'I'm going to miss my train.' It's not true. She has plenty of time, but she'd better get out of this situation before her heartbeat becomes unbearable.

'Can't we have a drink together somewhere downtown?' he asks. She says she's not used to expressions like 'let's have a drink' or 'I've been looking for you.' She stops, regretting it already.

'I'm sorry. I know I'm really rude sometimes.'

The new soldier on guard duty is staring at them.

'Let's move,' Ben proposes. 'You're not allowed to stand here for long. I'll walk with you wherever you're going. Let's sit down for five minutes, please.'

It's the first time she's ever sat in a café with a boy. Luckily the place is almost empty and this helps her behave more naturally. The café only offers dry-looking cakes and half-melted ice cream. Hana orders a lemonade that tastes like soda water while Ben has a cup of coffee.

'Finally,' he says, pleased with the way things are going. 'I didn't know who else to ask about you.'

This is a guy who doesn't give up, she thinks. He behaves like a one-man assault unit, but there's something about his manner that she likes. Ben's father is the dean of the medical school and his mother is a famous opera singer.

'Are you going to say something sooner or later?' he asks, with a smile. 'Or do I have to do all the work here?'

She's quiet, weighing her thoughts. 'Forget it, Ben,' she says, as kindly as she knows how. She's said his name. She goes red. 'It's a really bad time for me.'

He stares at her, his confidence draining away.

'I know I seem strange, but I'm not really. I know I look awkward, but I'm not really. Well, yes I am, a little, but that's not the problem right now. Right now I have to work out when I'm going to be able to cry. Then things will get easier. I can't cry right now, I really can't.'

He looks at her, even more confused. In the few films Hana has seen, the men look at their women exactly this way. The village doctor had looked at her that way at the *kulla*. Come on, explain it to him, she says to herself. Don't make him go away without even helping him understand. At least that.

She tells him that her uncle, Gjergj Doda, is dying of cancer and that he is the only person left in her family, except for a cousin her age called Lila who is married and doesn't live in the village anymore. Ben twirls the empty coffee cup around in his hand.

'I'm sorry,' he says.

They order again. This time Hana has a coffee and he asks for a little cake. He then asks if he can help in any way. She smiles without looking up and asks him if he can arrange things so that Uncle Gjergj doesn't die. He goes quiet.

'I have to go,' Hana says. 'Or I really will miss my train.'

'I wanted to be with you.'

'I wanted to be with you too,' she lets slip.

If he were less good-looking it would make things easier for her. And as for his voice . . .

Forget it, no way. Nothing.

'So stay,' Ben says. 'Stay until tomorrow.'

'I can't.'

She gets up and he follows her, after throwing the coins on the table to pay for their order. She doesn't even try to go through the useless routine of offering to pay. She knows he wouldn't allow it. She may as well save them both the whole song and dance.

Outside the café, the door closes behind them; the sun hanging like a sword over their heads, Hana holds out her hand and he takes it, tightening his grasp.

'My world is collapsing,' she says calmly, almost detached. 'And I don't know if I can hold it together. I don't even know why I'm telling you this. I need to go . . . '

Ben wants to walk her as far as the station, and does not take no for an answer.

They walk fast, heads down, in the vain attempt to shield themselves from the sun. She counts one and a half steps to every step of his. Hardly anyone else is walking outside. There are more bicycles made in China than anything else on Viale Stalin. Ben's legs are hidden in jeans; anyone who owns a pair of jeans in Tirana is rich and powerful. In front of the Variety Theater he asks her why her pants are white with salt. Hana tells him about her beach trip and how she didn't have a bathing costume.

'So you went swimming in your clothes?'

'I couldn't go in naked.'

'I did it once last year, it was cool.'

Hana laughs.

'When you don't have a change of clothes it's not so cool. My skin is stretched tight; there's no water at the dorm.'

'There isn't any at my place either. My mother's mad because she hasn't been able to use the washing machine for three days.'

She's heard from some of her classmates that he lives in Tirana's Eighth Quarter, a high-end residential area right next to where the Politburo members live.

They've reached the Science Faculty. Ben stops. People hauling suitcases and carry-on bags are rushing towards the entrance of the railway station.

'Can't you just stay today?' he begs her. 'We'll spend the day together. We've never had a chance to spend any time together alone, and we hardly know one another.'

Hana turns to him.

'I do know you. It's weird – and funny – but you seem familiar. There's something about you that somehow, somewhere, maybe in a dream, I've already come to know.'

Ben stuffs his hands in his pockets, takes them out, puts them back in again.

'You're an emotional roller coaster, you know? It's really hard to follow you. You confuse me, and make me feel insecure.'

'I know you,' she insists, taking no notice.

'I feel the same, but I can't just come out with things like that or I'd look like a liar or a jerk. Then you come out with them, you get there first, and you sound so convincing and natural that . . . '

They look away, trapped by their awkwardness, by the fact that they're young and have never been free.

'So stay, Hana. Before it's too late. Don't leave. I can't just lose you like this, for the whole summer.'

'I can't. Not today.'

'Can I come to your village then, maybe next week? Or when you say I can?'

'Are you crazy? Do you want to ruin me?'

'Why would it ruin you?'

'Because I'm from the mountains, Ben.' Hana has raised her voice. 'In the mountains men don't come and visit girls they're not engaged to. It's just not done.'

Ben thinks for a minute, visibly disconcerted.

'We could meet in secret then.'

Hana shakes her head.

'Things are different up there, the world doesn't work like you people in Tirana think it should.'

'I'm not "people in Tirana,"' he says, growing irritated. 'I'm Arben Leska, and that's all.'

'Don't get angry.'

'I'm not angry.'

'Yes you are, and so am I.'

'Where have you been hiding?' he challenges her, knowing it is useless. 'You vanished without trace when we'd just met.'

'What was I supposed to say?' Hana says, without any reproach. 'Was I supposed to ask a complete stranger for permission to go to my aunt's funeral? Was I supposed to say, "Wait for me until August, I might come back to school if Uncle Gjergj doesn't get worse. It's only a month and a half, can you wait that long?"'

She starts walking again, but he doesn't follow her. This is terrible, she thinks. You walk, then you stop, then you shout and then you'd like to hug him, and then you play hard to get, and then you lose him. You'll lose him. There won't be anything left in your life. He comes up to her. Hana waits.

'What I meant was that you vanished just when I decided I wanted to get to know you better. It's not easy to approach you, you know.'

'Well, now you've approached me and I'm not eating you alive.' Hana tries for a smile. 'We'll see each other at the end of August. You can wait until then, right?'

He takes a deep breath before spitting out that maybe at the end of August he'll be going to Paris. Her smile gets bigger. She hasn't understood.

'Maybe I'm going to Paris,' Ben repeats. 'I've won a scholarship. You heard the dean was compiling a list, right? There were four scholarships for French and I won one of them. They only told us a few days ago.'

She decides to cross the street. Easy does it. Easy. Don't be a fool. She shifts her bag to the other shoulder. Ben stands in front of her. She looks up.

'Good for you! I'm happy for you,' she mutters.

She's desperate for a way out that's quick and painless. For example, Ben turning around and leaving without a word. There's nothing to say. Everything in her life is going away, she says to herself. Everything is running away. Don't play the victim. Stop complaining. Stop.

'Have a good time, then.' She tries to soften the unpleasant tone of her voice. 'And good luck in Paris . . . Paris!'

'That's why I was in a hurry – and I didn't know how to find you.'

'I get it. Now I see.'

'How can I keep in touch, Hana? Is there anywhere I can call you in Rrnajë?'

'Sure! I have a phone in every room of my mansion.'

'Please, I don't want to lose you. We can keep in touch. I'll be coming to Albania in the summer, and even in the winter, maybe. We still have this month and a half to be together.'

'The train won't wait for me. I can't miss it.'

She runs. In seven or eight hours she'll be home, safe and sound. It's good to leave. There's something heroic about running away: you lose yourself, you fade away, you turn into a cloud, or maybe a man. You need courage to run away.

On the train she finds a seat with no upholstery and takes her place.

By the time she gets to Rrnajë she's exhausted. People in the village have brought food to Uncle Gjergj. Enver is bleating for his mistress and won't let Hana touch him. The sheep is as indifferent to her as ever.

One of these days Hana is going to have to go to the cooperative livestock pens and see how their cow is doing. Her name is Cow; they never gave her a proper name. When she lived at the Dodas', she was in great shape. Recently, she's looked terrible.

In their first decades in power, the communists had allowed families to keep one or two animals of their own. Then, with the new agricultural policies, the state had taken them away and things went from bad to worse. Now property is shared, and it is all managed by the agricultural cooperative, which means that, instead of working, the former owners sabotage state property. As soon as Cow started living in the state-owned stalls she stopped recognizing the Dodas, but they used to visit her anyway.

Hana washes, throwing water from a copper bucket over herself. She cooks dinner – the usual beans and potatoes with old brown bread – and they eat it in silence. Gjergj looks at her furtively and when their eyes meet he looks down.

'I thought you wouldn't come back,' he says, lighting his pipe.

'Where would I go, Uncle Gjergj?'

He is sitting up straight today; he looks almost healthy.

'I see it's done you good, me leaving you alone,' she teases. 'You look better now than when I left you. Maybe I shouldn't have come back.'

'What nonsense! What was it like down in Tirana?'

'Hot.'

'Did you enroll at school?'

'Sure.'

'Good job, dear Hana. You are the perfect son. Pity you were born a girl. If you were a boy, the *kulla* would have someone to take care of everything now.'

'Why? Aren't I taking care of everything as it is?'

'I'm talking about when I'm gone. I've been thinking about it a lot. If I don't marry you off now while I'm still alive, you'll end up without a husband and you know only a man can take care of everything. Maybe I've found the right person for you to marry. The day after tomorrow he'll be here.'

'Who will be here?'

'You heard me. Your future husband. I want to see you settled, I've decided. I can't leave you alone.'

Hana is silent.

'This is my duty,' he continues. 'You need someone to take care of you.'

She still doesn't say a word.

'I won't give you to the first man who comes along. I'll find you a good husband, with a diploma and a good family. Don't be scared: you'll finish school, come back here and be a high-school teacher. That will be my deal with the family. Until now I haven't taken anyone into consideration seriously because you wanted to go on studying. But things are different now.'

Hana gets up and goes out. She hears Uncle Gjergj's scratchy voice, too weak to stop her. She walks around the *kulla*. It's a beautiful night with a full moon. The garden is bathed in silvery light. Uncle Gjergj's pants are still hanging on the line where she left them three days ago.

It's all so cursedly beautiful: the perfume of the woods, the light breeze she feels ruffling her hair, the color of the night. She loves this place. They say nostalgia is only for the old; maybe she's already old. Maybe she was born old. She feels love for the night, which in her life never seems to end, but there is no bitterness. It's a fantastic feeling. It's the stuff of poets. Writers. And she is neither. Calm down and keep your feet on the ground, she says to herself. Don't get ahead of yourself, Hana; don't say things that sound crazy. You are normal, aren't you? She takes a deep breath and acts normal. You've just been threatened with marriage. Act scared.

No way. She doesn't feel any fear, or even anger. She goes on loving the moment, her breath, her calloused palms, her farmhand looks. She loves the courage she felt when she got up and left Uncle Gjergj inside and impotent. She managed to keep him under control.

When she goes back inside she tells Uncle Gjergj she will not accept any husband. He lies down. The pipe resting on the ashtray smokes itself.

'No husband. Do you see? I will not accept. If a future husband arrives the day after tomorrow, I'll run away. I don't want to be married and submit to the orders of a man, wash his feet, even. I will not be a slave.'

'You'll be left alone,' Gjergj says slowly. 'A woman who is not married is worth nothing.'

'Women are the same as men.'

'Like hell they are. Women are made to serve men and have children. Don't be a fool!'

She finds it hard to control her anger.

'I thought you were different,' she says through her teeth. She's not even sure he hears, because there is no reaction.

'You'll be alone in the world,' he repeats. 'But I won't leave you undefended.'

'You're still alive, Uncle Gjergj. I won't let you die.'

'You can't do anything about it.'

'You can't leave me. You're the only family I have.'

'That's what I mean. After I'm gone you can't remain here alone.'

'What do you know about it? Let me deal with it.'

Her uncle tries to smile.

'School has ruined you. You've turned into a city girl, and you've forgotten your position. I was wrong to let you go.'

She strides up to his bedside, snuffs his pipe out angrily and stares until he looks away.

'You're only a woman,' he says, upon a sudden, treacherous impulse, seeking to diminish her.

'And you're only a man,' she answers. He's old and finished, there's no hope. Aunt Katrina, you were so wrong.

She storms out of the house and slams the door, crying, shouting, suffocating.

'Die, you bastard,' she cries out into the night. 'I thought you were different. Just die!'

She tries to calm down, but it takes her a long time. God forgive my anger. But God doesn't exist in Rrnajë; it's a crime to invoke him. Priests are condemned by the regime; they are rotting in prison because they turned to God.

Much later, when she goes back into the *kulla*, Gjergj says sorry. He says he knows she's different, that she was always different, even when she was a little girl; that bringing her up was what kept him and poor Aunt Katrina alive, and that it's not true she is only a woman. She is Hana. And there will never be another Hana.

She moves closer to him. She can't believe her ears: a man never apologizes to a woman. She weighs Gjergj's words in her mind, examines him closely to make sure he isn't playing a trick on her. Then she says:

'So, no more talk of marriage?'

'If you're really sure, my little girl.'

'Yes, I'm really sure.'

'Well, promise me you'll take care of yourself when I die.'

'You're not going to die.'

'Promise me anyway.'

'I promise.'

'You'll be strong.'

'A rock.'

'You'll be the man of this house.'

'Go to sleep, now. If you sleep well, tomorrow I'll take you out to see the village.'

'I'd like that.'

'We'll go and see Aunt Katrina, and then we'll go to the square.'

'Hana, dear daughter, I'm so sorry.'

The next day the whole of Rrnajë is there to greet them, hands on their hearts: Gjergj, *bre burrë, a je?*

Uncle and niece visit Katrina's grave. Hana has brought fresh flowers. Gjergj stands motionless, dazzled by the pile of earth as if it were the sun.

'I'll remember this little jaunt, dear daughter,' he says later on.

When Gjergj's condition worsens, Hana hitches a ride into town in a truck. She telephones the clinic in Kavajë where the village doctor now works and he promises to send her some painkillers to help Gjergj suffer less.

'You should really take him to hospital,' he tells her. 'They'd be able to take better care of him.'

The phone line sounds weary, as if they are on opposite sides of the world.

'If you come to Tirana, get in touch. We could meet, if you feel like it.'

The phone line groans. He waits and so does she.

'Hana,' the doctor says, 'I have to go. I'm with a patient right now.'

'Of course, sure.'

'Take your uncle to the hospital and then run away from that village of yours. Come to Tirana and finish school. You have your whole future ahead of you.'

Through the dirty glass of the phone box Hana observes the filthy Scutari post office, where people are waiting impatiently for a free phone booth to slip into so that the world doesn't forget all about them.

'Will you listen to me, Hana? You can't save him, and you can't bury yourself alive with him.'

'Thank you for everything, Doctor,' she says, pleased with the tone of voice she manages to produce, while the dirty glass helps her feel protected for a little while longer; for as soon as she leaves the phone booth, she'll be just like all those people waiting outside, unwashed, undernourished, badly dressed, worlds apart from French women.

'You can't bury yourself up in the mountains,' the doctor repeats, as if she were deaf.

Gjergj will never agree to go back to the hospital and be hitched up to the machines again. He has chosen his path. He wants to die in his own bed, and Hana agrees with him. She'll keep him company until the end. She'll be right there beside him, more for herself than for him. How can you explain certain things? These things? Everything? It's impossible to explain to somebody on the other end of a crippled phone line in a crazy country.

There's no need to explain anything, as it turns out, because the phone line goes dead. For both of our sakes, Hana thinks, as she steps out of the phone box into the glaring and restless sun that still doesn't know what it wants to be when it grows up.

The village nurse comes and gives Gjergj his shots. Hana gives him his pills at regular intervals. One day she starts reciting poems to him without saying what they are. She recites a bit of everything, from Emily Dickinson to Walt Whitman, from Paul Éluard to Juan Ramón Jiménez, and, of course, her beloved Hikmet. Every now and then, alongside the great poets, she smuggles in some of her own poems. She waits to see if he reacts, trying to recite them with a different voice, playing with the stresses. I'm so pathetic, she thinks, but she can't help it, her need is too strong. Uncle Gjergj often falls asleep between one poem and the next; she will never know whether he liked them or not.

Cow dies in one of those scorching weeks. The vet from the agricultural cooperative climbs up to the Dodas' house to give them the news, and looks around.

'You must be hungry, young lady,' he says. 'What are you living on?'

'Sheep's milk, Comrade Veterinary Surgeon.'

'That's not enough.'

Hana smiles, confirming with her eyes.

'Tomorrow come to me and I'll give you a bit of flour, sugar and other stuff.'

Hana doesn't say that they don't have the money to pay and whatever money they do have goes on drugs for Uncle Gjergj.

'Ok,' she says instead. 'Thank you very much. I'll be there.'

She'll get by as well as she can, without begging for free food. Uncle Gjergj would be furious.

Uncle and niece spend the summer in a kind of truce, with the oncoming death looming over them.

On September 10, Arben Leska sends her a letter in which he says that he is about to leave for Paris.

At the end of the month, Gjergj gets up, and for a couple of weeks he seems better. He can't talk out loud and he can only swallow liquids, but he stands surprisingly upright. At times he even walks a bit. At other times he spends hours with Enver, at the door to the pen. One morning Hana hears him cursing the animal in a voice like sandpaper.

'You're a son of a bitch,' she hears him say. 'You've ruined our lives, you stupid billygoat.' Enver bleats away, unaware of the insults directed at him and unable to defend himself. His droppings land squarely on Gjergj's shoes.

It's a beautiful fall. Dawn takes its time turning into daylight, but the sunset is unwilling to concede to night. Everything is suspended, like a feather, or a breath, or a memory that doesn't want to be forgotten. And maybe Paris is make-believe, just like Gjergj's sickness.

When there is absolutely nothing left to eat in the house, Hana decides to ask for work at the agricultural cooperative. They give her a position cleaning the animal pens.

She sets off early in the morning and gets back home late in the evening every day for four weeks running, until one day she realizes that the number of ashtrays and grappa glasses scattered around the house means that a lot of people must have been there in her absence. She questions Gjergj but he denies having had visitors.

Their neighbor, old mother Rrokaj, confirms that Gjergj is about to host an engagement party in Hana's honor, and that her future husband is a man from a village on the Kosovo border. He's from a good family and, rather than taking Hana to his village, he has promised to move into the Dodas' *kulla* after Gjergj dies. He's an elementary-school teacher in his village and so he is educated, like Hana.

'You're a lucky girl,' the woman says. 'Your uncle is such a good man that he won't die before providing for you.'

For three days Hana stops eating and refuses to talk to Gjergj.

Down in Tirana, school has already started. Some of the girls in her dorm must have fallen in love, and her favorite desk in the Introduction to Linguistics class has probably gained an extra doodle or food stain.

On the second day of November, the snow comes. This year it is later than usual. She has to go to Scutari to get more drugs.

'Make sure I don't find anyone in the house when I get back,' she warns her uncle before setting off.

'You don't give orders to me, young lady.'

'And if I do, what will you do?'

It's one of those rare occasions when he has managed to stand up straight and tall, like a rock in the middle of the dark room.

'No betrothals or husbands while I'm away, Uncle Gjergj. That was the deal.'

'It was, but not anymore. The wedding will be at the end of the year.'

He is so thin that, for the first time ever, Hana finds him ugly. They stare at each other angrily, and then Gjergj softens a little, and tries to sit down. Hana doesn't make a move to help him.

'Don't make me hate you, I beg you,' she says.

'Just look at you! You're so tiny,' he says, clearly in pain. 'Help me, I need to sit down.'

She turns around and leaves the house, slamming the door as she goes. She starts walking through the snow that has started to settle unexpectedly. She only stops to look back at the *kulla* when she is far enough away not to be seen by her uncle, who must surely be looking out of the window. She hasn't even placed the soup that she cooked the night before where he can reach it for his dinner.

She finds a ride down to the city in a truck driven by a peasant with a southern accent. Hana gives him the fare and climbs in without thinking twice. The driver stinks of alcohol and cigarettes, but in the mountains all the men stink of alcohol and cigarettes, so she relaxes.

The driver asks her a question every now and then, which she answers in monosyllables.

'This evening I have to go back up your way,' the truck driver says when they are just outside Scutari, at the Rosafa castle. 'I'll unload the wood here and then go back up to the mountains to sleep so tomorrow I can bring down a new load. If you want I'll give you a lift back.'

They negotiate a time and a fare. The man seems as angry as she is and they say goodbye without looking each other in the eye.

By the afternoon, Hana's anger has dissipated. She'll go home and be a good daughter to the old man, she promises, not for the first time. For one more month everything will be all right. She'll give him his drugs and he'll say, 'Good girl, you're like a son to me.'

She eats two *byrekë* at a stand in the center, near the Rosafa Hotel. Then she drops in at the library and borrows three books to return next month. By the end of her day in town she's even in a good mood.

During the trip back, the truck makes slower progress than it did on its way down because of the snow, even though it is empty.

Hana tries to be a little more friendly and asks the driver if he has any children. He mumbles something. He must be seriously angry with someone in the city, or maybe at himself, and is as hostile as he was this morning, so she stops trying to be nice.

At one point they see a group of people waving their arms to stop the truck, but there's no way he's going to pick them up. Hana tries to tell him the truck is empty so he could give those people a ride, but he tells her to mind her own fucking business and leave him alone. For half an hour they don't say a word. Then, when it is completely dark outside, the man stops the truck, leaving the engine running.

'I got to take a piss,' he slurs. 'Back in a minute.'

When he climbs back into the truck, his pants are open. Hana doesn't realize at first. The man's words are disgusting enough. She listens because she has no choice. The man says she'd better let him have his way, and anyway it doesn't make any difference. Women don't go out on their own unless they're up for it. Hana is shocked by his rough language. She slips her hand into the jute sack at her feet just in time. Don't make a fuss, lady, I won't hurt you, we'll just have a little fun together. When he pushes himself onto her, Hana is ready with her knife and she plunges it into his chest. Aunt Katrina always used this knife to take the heads off their chickens. The man groans. Hana always takes the knife with her when she goes down to the city. She sharpens it without letting Uncle Gjergj see.

'You fucking bitch!'

She jumps out of the truck and runs into the trees beside the road.

'You fucking bitch! Peasant woman! Mountain bitch!'

She doesn't get home until the next day, wet with snow and dead tired. Uncle Gjergj is as white as a shroud. He hasn't slept a wink. He looks at her as if she were a ghost. He doesn't ask any questions, but bangs his stick over and over on the stone wall, on the table. He's no stronger than an ant. She can't see his face. He's curled up in the corner of the room, his head buried in his chest.

The following day, Hana rummages through Gjergj's clothes chest, at the same time asking herself what she is looking for. She finds his national costume and puts it on, still wondering what she is doing. She rolls the pants up at the waist and tries to keep them up by tightening the red waistband. What are you doing? She stares at the wall in front of her. She smiles at the stone, and feels sorry for it. The stone has never been kissed. She leans her forehead on it and rests there for a while.

When she goes downstairs and presents herself to Gjergj dressed as a man, her uncle is struck dumb. But all of a sudden his chin starts to twitch and, however tightly he locks his jaw, it is not enough to hold back his emotion.

It's November 6, 1986.

Hana scratches the date on the wall of the guest room. It takes her a good hour to do it properly.

When she has finished, she goes back to Gjergj. He passes her his rifle. She takes it and examines it closely. It has belonged to six generations of Doda clansmen. Gjergj has kept it oiled for thirty-six years. Hana is still standing awkwardly. Now what? she asks herself. Now what? Now nothing. Now there is nothing. What time is it now in Paris? She's supposed to sit like a man, with her legs crossed, she's supposed to smoke a pipe like Uncle Gjergj. She looks at the legs sticking out of her pants, like a ladybug's, she thinks. To postpone the moment when she has to sit like a man, she stays standing.

'Are you sure you want to take this step, dear daughter?'

'My name will be Mark. Mark Doda.'

The next day the news spreads around Rrnajë and the village is alive with gossip. The men will greet her as a man, and the women will avoid her eye.

She starts to keep a diary.

●

In the five months that follow, Hana takes care of Gjergj, the house, the animals, the memory of Katrina. She tries to make her gait heavier, more masculine. It'll take time. Every now and then she gives herself a break. 'There is no hurry,' she tells herself.

Don't run, don't make a noise, don't think. There's no hurry. Not anymore. There's all the time in the world, nobody is waiting for you. You don't have to worry anymore about how soft your hair is; you don't have to worry about finding nice clothes; a world's worth of snow separates Rrnajë from Paris.

Now you're a man. You're a man. A man! You're not allowed to look at real men anymore.

Everything is just fine, she makes herself believe. The snow, the dark nights, the dogs chasing each other, the shadows of the wolves across the snowy landscape, hurrying like busy travelers. The mountains protect you and overwhelm you. The echo of centuries rings in your heart. They save you from the greasy panting of redneck truck drivers.

The memory is still alive. The terror she had felt. The night she had spent in the woods, her teeth chattering with the fear that, having escaped from one man with his pants open, another would suddenly appear from behind one of those trees.

She hadn't slept a wink. She had sharpened the darkness with her night eyes. If anybody had approached her she would have killed him. She had kept her knife close to her chest and her heart had never stopped beating furiously. She had been famished, she had been angry, she had called to her mother by her beautiful name; she had even invoked her father, whose face she couldn't remember.

She had prayed to God, and with mute tears; to the same God who had been banned a year before Hana was born and whom Felicità had always talked about in secret.

She had managed not to freeze to death. At dawn she had crept through the alleys of Rrnajë without being seen, protected by the snow. When she got home, the *kulla* had become hard as a rock. A grave for her old self. She had become a man.

'Honor to you for what you have done,' Gjergj's guests repeat in the months that follow. He is proud of her. You can see it in his eyes, which refuse to surrender to death, and in the way he passes Hana the bottle of raki.

'Gjergj, *bre burrë* now you have a son and the honor of the *kulla* will not die.'

Hana learns to smoke with them. She stinks like them. She copies their laughter and makes her voice more gravelly. Her throat and ribs hurt.

The whole of the Bjeshkët e Namuna – all the 'cursed mountains' – knows by now that the Dodas' daughter has become a man.

Some of the village men fire volleys of rifle shots to celebrate the event, and the man from the Party does not say a thing. Nor does the policeman. If things stay within limits, the Party is magnanimous. If a young girl decides to become the man of the house, well, traditions are to be respected. Within limits. Within *certain* limits.

One day Lila, her only first cousin, comes to Rrnajë with Shtjefën, her young husband, to visit her parents. She looks at Hana as if she has flown in from Mars.

'Hana, sweetie, what have you done? You of all people?'

Lila looks like a sheep. Her terrible perm makes her hair as fluffy as an old woman's. It's traditional: young wives curl their hair using an iron heated on the fire.

'Look at yourself; you look like a grandmother.'

'Why did you do it, Hana?'

'Your hair makes you look like an old lady. Your head-scarf makes you look like an old lady.'

'I'm married now.'

'That's pretty obvious.'

'Look, I love Shtjefën and I didn't walk down the aisle like a lamb to slaughter. He's a good man, he's not like the others.'

'But you wait on him without saying a word, and you let your in-laws tell you what to do, don't you?'

'What do you mean? It's tradition. There are such things as rules. Why did you do it, Hana?'

They observe each other. Lila waits for an answer, which Hana doesn't provide.

'You were shaping up to be a great young woman, you could have been a schoolteacher, and now . . . '

'Call me Mark,' she says to her cousin, hugging her so as not to be overwhelmed by tears.

'You're crazy,' Lila says, disoriented. 'You're totally crazy, Hana.'

Gjergj dies on a sunny May day in 1987. Everything is ready. The house is full of food, considering what little there is up in the mountains. The honor of the Doda family is more secure than ever. Mark receives condolences. Men and women show him equal respect. Nobody calls her Hana any longer.

The *kulla* is squeaky clean. Old habits die hard, and she struggles to neglect the housework. But she is trying. Men don't do women's work; that's the rule of the Kanun.[9]

A week after the funeral, Hana weeps in front of the pile of fresh earth that is Gjergj's grave. She is alone, so nobody will see her crying.

She cries for a long time, and then looks up at the clear blue sky, the bare cemetery, the small stretch of Rrnajë that extends beyond the graveyard. The sun is so warm and reassuring, it makes her feel as though she's on the top of the world.

On a day like this, her mother would have started singing.

DECEMBER 2001

Shtjefën gets home a little earlier than usual, and in a good mood. Lila is due back in half an hour. Jonida is doing her homework.

'I got you a job,' he says to Hana. 'The interview is tomorrow. See what you can do. They'll give you a two-week trial and then they'll decide. You'll be a daytime attendant at a parking lot near the subway station.'

Hana is surprised, and thanks him.

'I know you don't like being dependent on us,' he adds apologetically. 'And I didn't do it to put pressure on you if you don't feel up to it . . . '

Hana has cooked dinner, which they will eat at around seven thirty, when Lila gets back. Usually she rushes in and changes out of her work clothes, tearing them off as fast as she can. She takes a quick shower and then they have dinner.

Hana quit smoking a few weeks ago and is still coughing up phlegm. Shtjefën called her a traitor. Jonida is happy: 'Go for it, Hana! Show Mr Fatso that he can stop poisoning himself!' Mr Fatso smiles and readily accepts his daughter's affectionate insults.

'My Jonida is going to be an educated woman,' he says with infinite pride. 'She's beautiful and intelligent, and women like that can get away with saying a few words too many.'

That day, before Jonida and Shtjefën get back home, Hana tried on a skirt, which, Lila had explained, was called a tube skirt. It was made of dark fabric and it was the only skirt that Hana had agreed to buy during these three months.

With the house to herself she held a kind of dress rehearsal. She studied herself in the mirror for a long time – and found herself ridiculous. She walked up and down without taking her eyes off the mirror. And she did her best to resist the temptation to throw the skirt out of the window.

Jonida is home before Shtjefën. Hana closes her eyes as she throws open the door.

'Wow!' her niece shrieks, as she throws her backpack into a corner of the living room. 'Cool! Turn around, Hana!'

Hana obeys.

'I don't like the color,' Jonida says. 'Who chose it?'

'Apart from the color?'

'I said you look ok. It looks better from the front than from the back.'

Jonida rushes to the fridge to grab a low-fat yogurt.

'What is that stuff? Why don't you eat something more nutritious?'

'I hate cellulite.'

'You don't have cellulite, sweetie, but if you only eat this stuff you'll get too thin.'

'It's cool to be thin and you know it. Anyway, you look cute in the skirt, but you look better in pants.'

Hana hangs her head in disappointment. Jonida finishes her yogurt and throws the teaspoon in the sink. Hana rushes to rinse it. She adores Jonida's messiness; it keeps her busy during the day.

'You're weird,' the girl says, rubbing salt in the wound. 'You're flat behind. You have no backside.'

'Thanks.'

'It's my role isn't it? You asked me to be straight with you.'

'For weeks you go on at me, girly this, girly that, and then, first try, you put me down!'

'I love you. But if you're weird, you're weird, and I can't do anything about it.'

'I'll take it off, then.'

'You better not!'

Hana doesn't understand what's going on.

'We have to work at it, we can't just give up. You can't turn sexy in a day. Your face is already much better.'

'I don't want to be sexy, I've told you a thousand times,' Hana insists nervously. 'I just want to be normal and acceptable.'

'You want to be more than normal, Hana. You want to look good, and don't deny it.'

Hana sits on the sofa longing for a cigarette.

'How was school today?' she asks, changing the subject.

'Fine. I think the guy I like is with another girl. A friend told me today in the cafeteria.'

'Is this girl cute?'

'She's ugly as hell.'

Hana laughs with gusto.

'You're saying that because you're jealous,' she ribs.

'Me? Jealous?' Jonida's hair flies around her as she shakes her head. 'I am way better than her. Things like that don't get to me, but she's just plain ugly.'

Hana watches her. She has lived with Jonida for three months and, despite the intimacy they have created, she still finds things difficult. She envies her naturalness, the way Jonida is so accepting of her place in the world.

'I have to do my homework now, I've got a ton of things to do,' Jonida announces, jumping up and skipping into her bedroom.

Hana sits on the sofa lost in thought until Shtjefën

gets back home, but she does decide one thing: not to take off the skirt.

'The job won't be too tiring,' Shtjefën says. He looks up and notices the change in her. 'Finally! Lila will be pleased to see you like this.'

They both smile.

'I don't want an easy job,' Hana says. 'I want a job where I get really tired and where I can learn the language.'

'But you're doing great, what are you worrying about? I wish I could speak English as well as you!'

Just then Lila gets home. She hangs her bag in the hall, mumbles a worn-out, drawling 'hi,' goes and takes a shower, and comes back into the kitchen with her hair still wet.

Casting her eyes over the kitchen stove and the table set for four, she tosses an inquisitive 'so?' into the air and then adds, 'What have you made for dinner, Hana?'

Just then Lila notices and her eyes light up.

'Stand up! Stand up now! I wish I'd been here when you were putting that skirt on, for crying out loud. You've been driving me crazy all this time. Stand up!'

Shtjefën goes out. Hana just stands there, her arms hanging limply by her sides.

'You look great. Walk around a bit . . . '

Hana slumps back into her chair.

'Come on, don't start being difficult! Let me see you! This is a historic moment. Now you are a woman from every point of view.'

You make it sound easy, Hana thinks, without taking her eyes off the empty plates. She wants to eat, clean the table, and go out for her usual stroll.

'Are you happy?'

'Yes, I'm fine. Tomorrow Shtjefën is taking me to my first job interview.'

'He found you a job? And you don't even tell me? We have to celebrate!'

Jonida comes out of her bedroom. Lila turns, bounds towards her, and wraps her daughter in a greedy embrace.

'Oh my darling! Light of my eyes! How are you, my love?'

'Take it easy,' she says. 'You're squishing me. We saw each other this morning, Mom, remember?'

Lila has no intention of letting go. Shtjefën comes back into the room and gently, almost shyly, hugs his wife and daughter. They are so beautiful and there's no need for anything else, there's no need for words or dreams or memories. All I need to do is be here and smile, Hana says to herself. And she smiles, looking at these three people who have adopted her but from whom she can't wait to escape.

Jonida turns to her father and rubs her nose against his chin.

'Hi, big Daddy bear,' she says to him. 'Is everything ok?'

'Everything is fine, my love. What about you?'

They do not let go, none of the three wants to separate,

they stroke each other. Hana goes on smiling, but her smile becomes a lump in her throat and a grimace of pain crosses her face.

'Ok, that's enough for now.' Jonida throws herself down on the sofa, next to Hana.

'I'm hungry.'

Lila goes into the kitchen and takes the lid off the saucepan. Hana makes an effort not to cry, but she can't stop. She runs into the bathroom.

She remembers the day her parents hugged each other in front of her. They were standing. Her mother was beautiful; her father had surrendered to his wife's sweetness. Hana had watched them closely. They had embraced in front of their daughter the day before they got onto the bus that was supposed to take them to their cousin's wedding in the city.

The bus had ended up at the bottom of a ravine that winter afternoon and no one was able to reach the wreck. They were buried in the snow that fell that night and slept in ice until the following spring. When they recovered the bodies, they found her mother's red and blue headscarf and her father's pipe.

Since then Hana has kept these treasures with her. She brought them here and has them stashed in her suitcase under her bed.

Dinner is delicious. Hana has taken a lot of trouble choosing the menu. She's trying to learn to cook. She has even bought a cookbook and this evening she has prepared green salad with raisins, spaghetti with meat sauce, and baked apples.

'It was all delicious,' Lila encourages her after polishing off the last mouthful of apple. 'Really delicious.'

Shtjefën offers to make Turkish coffee.

'Tomorrow will you take me for a drive?' Hana asks them. 'I'd like to get a little driving practice, to get used to the traffic.'

They sip their coffee.

'I miss my old truck,' she continues. 'And if all goes well at work, in a month I'd like to start looking for a small apartment, Lila.'

She waits for a reaction. Shtjefën gets up to make more coffee. Jonida winks at Hana. Lila is quiet for a moment.

'I didn't realize you were in such a hurry to get away,' she says.

'I'm not in a hurry to get away. I just want to see if I can live on my own.'

'But you've lived on your own for fourteen years!'

Lila is taking it badly, Jonida can see it in her face. But Hana is already at the door:

'I'm going out for a walk.'

She throws a jacket on over her t-shirt and shuts the door, leaving behind the confused rancor of her cousin. It's not cold; this winter is mild, the evening a little damp. She takes the path she now knows by heart. Her shoes are comfortable; she doesn't like them particularly but they were cheap.

Lila is a great bargain-hunter. She runs the household finances confidently, hunting out special offers and discounts. On Thanksgiving Day, she got up at four in the morning and drove all the way to the big supermarket outside town that was famous for its unbeatable prices. She came back four hours later, exhausted but happy, with three gigantic shopping bags. Fifteen minutes to put everything away in the fridge and she had climbed back into her car, this time with Hana and Jonida, to buy clothes for Jonida at the store where she worked.

Hana stops. The skirt is annoying her. It's too wide in the waist and the zipper at the back keeps making its way to the front. She tugs the skirt round and starts walking again. A few yards on, the skirt has twisted again. She suddenly feels a strange sensation on her legs. Last week she tried shaving them. She also shaved her armpits and then spent days itching and scratching. Jonida nearly died laughing. She kept an eye on the hairs that were growing back on her legs. Before putting the skirt on, she had shaved again, nicking herself slightly with the razor. She stops again. The skirt won't stay put. Trying to keep walking, she stumbles, though without actually falling over. At that, she makes up her mind to go back, and walks home in furious strides.

Shtjefën is watching TV and Lila is doing whatever she does in the bathroom. A deep hammering bass beat comes from Jonida's bedroom. Hana slips silently into Lila and Shtjefën's room and tears off her skirt. She scrunches it up, venting all her anger on it. Then she crumples it into a ball, opens the wardrobe and throws it inside.

'What are you doing?' Lila asks from the doorway.

Hana thrusts her legs into her pants as fast as she can.

'You are out of this world,' her cousin says. 'Just try and understand someone like you.'

'And you are as clingy as a shadow.'

Hana leaves the house again. She thought everything would be easier. When she had become Mark she had had no real experience of femininity. And now she's even scared about her job interview tomorrow. Her English sucks.

'You have to look confident,' Shtjefën coaches her. 'Americans always look incredibly self-confident. They like to look sure of themselves. Don't talk about your problems and you'll be fine. Then you can fall apart when you're on your own.'

She is excited and lost at the same time. On the outside she looks almost like a woman. What's missing is her vision, the point of view from which she is supposed to read the world. When she observes people, Hana does not see a woman or a man. She tries to penetrate the unique spirit of the individual, she analyzes their face and eyes, she tries to imagine the thoughts hiding behind those eyes, but she tends to avoid thinking about the fact that these thoughts are inextricably linked to the male or female ego. Women think like women. Men? Well, the answer is obvious. She's only just realizing now that for a long time she has had to consider things from both points of view.

On the other hand, she consoles herself, the diaries that she kept during her years as Mark are not that badly written. In her days by herself in Rockville she has read them again and again. She is also sorry to realize that her diaries are better than her poems. This thought has no particular value, but it hurts all the same. She would have liked to be a poet.

She reads a lot. Shtjefën teases her, saying that, in order to satisfy Hana's requests, they will soon have to ask for new funding at the Rockville city library. The librarians have been very helpful; they give her advice and encourage her. Hana fills whole notebooks with words and idiomatic expressions and learns them off by heart. She watches programs on TV late into the night to improve her English. Talking to Jonida is the best practice of all, because her vocabulary is peppered with adolescent slang.

Lila can't understand why she is going to such trouble.

'There's no point,' she says. 'You don't need perfect English to be a parking attendant or a cleaning lady. All you're trying to do is to become a woman, not a PhD or whatever it's called.'

'Without language you can't do anything,' Hana answers.

'Ok, keep on dreaming, just like when you were nineteen. You're wasting time on books, instead of worrying about your appearance.'

They argue, then they make up, then they argue again and sometimes don't call a truce for two days. To the point that, every day, when she gets in from school, Jonida asks them how their daily fight has gone.

'It's too late for your dreams, Hana,' Lila sighs with exhaustion. 'Why don't you listen to me? Years back you should've done what we all did: get married, have children. You would have had a hard time, of course. Every woman has her share of suffering. But you thought you were better than us, and you rebelled and now here you are. It's too late for impossible dreams.'

Hana smiles bitterly, saying so helpful, Lila, really encouraging.

'I just tell you things as they are.'

'But it is not the way things are.'

'Ok, you tell me then, come on. You tell me how and what you're going to do in this country, because I've been living here for ten years and yet somehow you seem to know it better than me even though you just got off the boat.'

'Fine Lila, you're right.'

'Don't be so condescending!'

'Ok.'

'Even though I don't read stacks of paper, I'm not stupid.'

'It's not paper, Lila, it's my soul. Books are my soul.'

'Stop talking fancy. I'm beat.'

Hana's arms are crossed over her breasts. She's wearing a pretty white lace bra. Lila shouts and shouts.

'Be patient,' Hana says to her, later on. 'As soon as I get a job, I will leave you in peace.'

'That is such a bitchy thing to say, I can't believe it. It just goes to show you really want to hurt me. That's not what I wanted to say. I don't want to force you to leave.'

'I know.'

'So don't say it again.'

'I am the one that wants to leave,' Hana says, gently. 'You're nothing to do with it, none of you have anything to do with it. You have been wonderful to me, but I want my independence. If I manage to start living again it will only be from that starting point.'

'I'm not even listening to you.'

'Do as you like.'

'You are so self-obsessed, it's unbelievable. There, that's what I think of you.'

'Fine.'

'Stop saying "fine," ok? You are no better than me!'

Lila gets up, tears her apron off and thrusts her copy of the *Washington Post*, which Hana had been reading before they started arguing, onto the floor.

'You are totally and utterly self-obsessed, I'll say it again, and I don't care one bit if it hurts you! All of us women back there in the mountains were basically workers and available bodies for our husbands; no one ever asked us our opinion, and we always obeyed. You hid yourself away instead of fighting for your cause. You became a man. Surprise, surprise, you took the easy choice! It's easy to be a man! The real problem out there was being a woman, not being the usual jackass who kills himself with alcohol and tobacco.'

Shtjefën puts his head round the door. Lila's words are lying there, dead, on the floor. Hana feels tears rise up in her throat. Shtjefën covers his eyes with his hands.

'Lila, baby, you'll wake the neighbors.'

Hana goes to drink a glass of water. Then she turns towards her cousin and stares at her, trying to catch her eye.

'And what do you know, Lila?' she retorts quietly. 'What do you know about what it means to be a man up there in the mountains? So only you women suffered? Is that what you really think? You think you women know everything about everything?'

She is unable to keep back her tears. Big tears.

'I'm sorry, Lila, I didn't want to ruin your life,' she adds.

'You haven't ruined it, how many times do I have to tell you?' Lila protests in vain. 'I want to see you happy. I want to see you settled. I care about you as much as if you were my Jonida. But you are so strange, you're not one thing or another, and when I see you wasting time with your books my blood pressure shoots up.'

Shtjefën sighs deeply.

'Of all places, I had to end up in this hen-house, for Christ's sake?' He laughs, his voice thick with sleep.

Hana is thankful he has woken up, otherwise who knows how things would have ended up with Lila this time.

Her cousin is full of resentment. It's a sentiment without ill will, but it is tiring her out. Lila wanted to become a nurse but she is a cleaning lady. She wanted to be well off but she is forced to hunt for bargains and work all hours just to break even, and so that Shtjefën doesn't have to work overtime when his seventy-hour week is already weighing on him. Lila pretends to be happy, but she is not a very good actress. The fact that she is now an American is no longer enough for her. The sacrifices she has made are sapping her energy, but she can't bear anyone to point it out.

'If you really want to help me,' Hana says finally, 'let me go.'

After that day there are no more arguments.

Jonida is already excited about the idea that maybe one day Hana will have a place of her own.

'It's so cool! I'll have two homes!' she brags at every opportunity. 'I'll come over to your place on the weekend, Hana. We'll be crazy together.'

Christmas is coming and Lila wants it to be memorable. The whole clan is going to be getting together.

'I want it to be a perfect day for all of us,' she keeps saying. 'You're going to get a facial,' she says to Hana, one day. 'And that's an order.'

One morning, Lila drags her to the beauty parlor. Hana lets her do it because she can't stand the idea of any more arguments. After her facial her skin is soft and smooth.

'You're so beautiful,' Lila exclaims as she emerges. 'All we need to do now is wait for your hair to grow out a little, give it a nice shape, and then we're done.'

They are in front of the beauty parlor.

'You do know all about sex and stuff, don't you?' Lila asks her out of the blue.

'What are you asking me? I think I know.'

'Back then, when you were in Tirana, did you ever do it?'

'No.'

'You mean you're totally a virgin?'

'No, just half!' Hana laughs out loud. 'I know what you have to do in theory, if that's what you mean.'

Lila breathes a sigh of relief.

'Good,' she says, and then adds, in the tone of a naval officer, 'but we need to talk about it. I bet there are many things you don't know.'

Hana objects that usually she's pretty good at theory, but Lila silences her by saying that only practice can give you the full picture.

'In books they write about sex all the time,' Hana says. 'And I have to say I like the sex scenes quite a lot.'

Lila thinks about this for a while.

'Did you know there's such a thing as do-it-yourself sex?' she asks, all in one breath.

Hana knows.

'You've never tried it?'

'No, never,' she lies, a patch of red creeping up her neck, but Lila is turning the ignition and doesn't look at her.

Her evening walk is longer than usual; she knows she won't be able to get to sleep tonight. The darkness is mild, languid and loaded with exhaust fumes. The traffic is intense, though it is late.

If she gets the job, she'll soon have a bit of privacy. In her new apartment she'll try again to make love on her own. Not now, not in Lila's house. There's something that holds her back there.

The one and only time she had tried she was still in the mountains, and it hadn't gone too well. She had cried for days afterwards.

After this thought she finds it hard to continue her stroll calmly. At College Plaza, rather than turning left down College Parkway, she turns around and goes back home.

•

The man who interviews her for the job is a fifty-year-old from Nicaragua who speaks faltering English, which makes Hana a little more relaxed. He explains that she will have to check the cars as they come into the parking lot and give them a ticket to put on their windscreens. Then, when they go out, she'll have to take the ticket back and get the money. She'll have to keep the cash register in order, and keep track of the daily cash flow. And she'll also have to make sure cars don't park in the spaces reserved for monthly season-pass holders. If they do, she'll have to call the towing company and have them removed.

Hana is sitting rigidly on the edge of her chair and can't seem to find a position in which she would look more natural. The guy from Nicaragua runs three parking lots like this one.

'During your working hours, you are in charge of the lot,' the man tells her. 'The first funny business you try, you're out. Is that clear? It's the first time I've hired a woman as an attendant – for obvious reasons I'd prefer a man. But Steven is my cousin's boss at the street maintenance company, and my cousin says he's a great guy, so that's why I'm giving you the job. It's up to you now: if you work as hard as he does, we'll both be happy. That's it, Hana. Call me Paco. My name is Francisco, but everyone calls me Paco.'

Shtjefën is waiting outside. Paco asks her if she speaks any Spanish. Hana shrugs: no.

'Pity. If you have problems with English, a bit of Spanish will always save you around here. But your English is more than enough for what you need to do. Today you'll be on trial, and for the first four hours there'll be one of my guys here to teach you everything you need to know. His name is Jack.'

Hana thanks him and goes outside, followed by her new boss. She feels drained. Shtjefën exchanges a few words with Paco, then tells Hana he has to leave her now to go to work. He'll be back to pick her up at around seven, but she shouldn't worry if he's late, it'll just depend on the traffic.

He leaves.

Hana has a kind of good-luck charm in her pocket. It's a stone from Rrnajë with a hole in the middle. She strokes it without taking it out of her pocket.

'Hana,' Paco calls out to her, 'Jack's here.'

Jack is black and rough looking, and very kind. Unfortunately he expresses himself in incomprehensible slang. She asks him shyly to speak more slowly because she's new to the country, but he says sadly he can't speak any other way. He asks her what her name is. She says Hana, but when he repeats it the 'a' turns into an open, nasal 'e.' Hana explains that she really cares about the way her name is pronounced; she wants him to get it right. He stops chewing his gum for a moment, looks at her with a curious expression, and smiles.

As the day goes by, she begins to appreciate Jack. He tells her a lot about himself, though she only understands half of it. At the end of the four hours he holds out his hand, shakes hers hard, says they will see each other that evening, and leaves.

Hana breathes in the unhealthy air of the parking lot. It has three floors, two of which are underground. She has the sensation of a breeze blowing through her brain. One by one, in her mind she goes over the things Jack has shown her.

'I'm sorry for your sake,' Jack had said twice during the final half hour of her training. 'You'll be on your own here. It's the only thing about this job I don't like. If I can't talk to someone, I go crazy.'

Hana told him that for her it wasn't a problem.

'You're only saying that because you have no idea what it means not to talk for hours at a time.'

The day of the shooting competition at Rrnajë, Mark Doda had been caressing the stone with the hole in the middle intensely. It was always in the same right-hand pocket. The men had been noisy. Senseless, Mark had thought, all this was senseless, over the top; their senseless words the result of senseless excitement. Lul, the owner of the scruffy café in the village, had suggested starting with the easiest targets, middle-sized stones perched on bigger rocks. The shooting was to be only with Kalashnikovs; every *kulla* had more than one in the house. In Tirana they had broken into the military arsenals. The whole of Albania had gone crazy, shooting wildly in the streets. In two months it would be 1998. Weapons traveled through Montenegro and Kosovo all the way to Serbia, and the 'cursed mountains' happened to be in their path.

The café owner had suggested a shooting competition rather than firing like crazy at nothing in particular like those idiots in Tirana. They had chosen a clearing near the village, in a narrow gorge. After each round they had drunk a shot of raki. The first round had been on Lul, but then they all had to pay their way. The targets had grown smaller and smaller.

Mark had been sweating, but had continued to caress his secret amulet. It had gone surprisingly well, considering. He had been eliminated more than halfway through the competition and was amazed he had made it that far. Shkurtàn, from the Gjetaj clan, had won. When it was all over, and silence had enveloped the mountains once more, the air had reeked of gunpowder and raki.

The men had collapsed on the ground or slumped in broken chairs, soaked in their melancholy, until deep into the night. The day after, the village kids had gathered up the cartridge cases; and the boys in the Gjetaj clan had enjoyed a few weeks of glory thanks to Shkurtàn's skill with an automatic. Then, yet again, there had been the usual emptiness.

Hana is smiling, sitting all alone in the cramped guardian's office. Remembering herself as Mark, whatever else it makes her feel, can't not give her pleasure. She even smiles at Jack, just like that, without saying a word. The world is at her feet. Less than three months have gone by since she left Rrnajë and here she is, thanks to Shtjefën, with a job. She's so happy that, if she could, she would give herself a big hug.

If the job is like this first day then everything will be ok. She just needs to pay attention. She needs to be hard-working, punctual. Not be scared of the language. Speak to the drivers when they want to know things, pronouncing every word carefully. Not be in a hurry. She's new to the country, and she can say so without raising any red flags, Lila has explained over and over. In America having just arrived is no big deal. In Europe you're immediately labeled inferior, especially in Central and Eastern Europe. If you say you're Albanian you're toast. America's much better from this point of view. It's tough for newcomers, but the Americans are so used to foreigners they hardly take any notice. And then they don't pry into your private life. No questions asked. They're always going someplace else in a hurry, and they mind their own business. Hana likes the part about minding their own business more than all the rest put together.

A high-powered car is pulling into the half-empty parking lot. The woman driving is massively overweight and Hana catches herself thinking she will find it hard to get out of the vehicle. She gives her the entrance ticket, which the woman puts on her dashboard. So far, so good.

The day goes by without incident, marked by nothing other than cars coming in and cars going out. Hana irons out the crumpled, mostly one-dollar bills with her hands and puts them into tidy piles. She goes over everything three times, just to be extra sure.

Jack comes back to pick up the day's earnings. The guy doing the night shift is with him. From Poland originally, he speaks in monosyllabic grunts. If he were a bit friendlier, she might even tell him she's Albanian – after all, they were once in the same communist bloc – but the guy clearly has no intention of starting a conversation.

Hana waits for Shtjefën to come pick her up on the sidewalk, leaning on a streetlight. It's a cold evening. It has suddenly become winter. She focuses on the sneakers she's wearing for the first time today. They're white and blue and go well with her dark-blue suit and white shirt. The shirt has a left breast-pocket with a pink border. Hana strokes the stitching as she waits.

Shtjefën pulls up in front of her. Hana could easily

get a bus home. It was only a few stops, but Lila and Shtjefën insisted.

'Hop in,' he calls out to her. 'Have you been waiting long?'

She climbs in, a bit distracted.

'Is everything ok?' Shtjefën asks her. 'Why didn't you wait at the bar instead of standing here getting cold? You had money with you, right?'

'Everything's fine. It was easy.'

'I told you so.'

Shtjefën pulls away from the curb, his tires squealing. He needs a haircut and some rest, she thinks, so she decides to keep quiet.

He doesn't stop at home, but carries on driving without any explanation. In Gaithersburg he announces that they're on their way to buy her a used Honda.

'The son of one of my workers owns a small garage, and he's giving us a great price on a car that was headed for the junkyard.'

'Does Lila know about this?'

'She'd tie you to the bed rather than see you go. We need to present her with a fait accompli. I'll pay, for now. You can pay me back when you have the money.'

'Lila's not going to like it.'

'Your cousin is very understanding. You just have to know how to handle her,' Shtjefën says with a sly smile. 'And I know how to handle her.'

Hana is so happy she's ashamed of it. Her left breast is itching. This is too much all in one day.

'Shtjefën, I'm . . . '

'Relax,' he says, interrupting her. 'And stop thanking me. I can't take it anymore, all day it's thank you this and thank you that. Have pity on me!'

Less than an hour later, Hana is the proud owner of a white Honda, which she drives home extremely cautiously, tailing Shtjefën. When they get home, Jonida lets out a shrill 'Wow!' Lila looks sad but content. Hana says she's going to buy four steaks from Whole Foods and there's no way the family can stop her, though they never shop there. It's a place for rich people who only eat organic, and the prices are way too high.

Hana pats the Maryland drivers' license in her pocket, leaps into the twelve-year-old Honda, and takes off. She comes back with meat and salad, wine from another store, and two packs of cigarettes. She spends nearly 100 dollars.

That evening she eats, drinks, and smokes, and even Jonida seems to have very little to say about it. At around eleven, her niece falls asleep and Lila has to take her to bed. Hana has knocked back so much that she feels as drunk as a lord. When she ends up in the bathroom with her head in the toilet bowl, her cousin doesn't dare go and help her.

'I'm sorry, Lila. It won't happen again,' Hana says the next morning, before leaving for work.

She parks in her reserved spot. For the rest of the day she feels foolishly proud of herself.

When she gets back home, she still has a headache. She decides to devote her evening to a map of Maryland. One day she'd like to drive as far as Annapolis, the state capital, and see a bit of Chesapeake Bay.

Shtjefën and Lila are at the movies in Rockville.

'They're like honeymooners,' Jonida comments. 'God save us from these old romantics!' But she's secretly happy for them, and kissed them both on the forehead as they left.

Auntie and niece spend no more than an hour together. Hana asks Jonida to explain a few things about the computer to her. Just the basics, she insists. But she is slow to pick it up and things need repeating. Jonida grumbles. Perhaps it's for the best, Hana thinks. I'll learn in my own time. She's happier on her own. Since she left the mountains, she misses her solitude. In the old days she would have done anything to have a bit of company. Now she feels her life is over-crowded.

JUNE 2002

It's Thursday. Summer has come with a vengeance, asphyxiating in its humidity. Hana has not touched alcohol in six months, since she got drunk on her first day of work. Tonight, however, she decides to buy a bottle of wine. She hurriedly steps out of the studio apartment she rented three weeks ago. It's noisy and cramped, overlooking the chaotic traffic of the Rockville Pike, and fifteen minutes from Lila and Shtjefën's place. It's 600 dollars a month, two months' deposit hands down. She signed a contract, which made her anxious. Pages and pages of quibbling articles full of legal terms that sent her running for her dictionary to look them up with meticulous diffidence.

In the neighborhood store, the young salesperson short-changes her by five dollars. She demands her correct change and he apologizes. Hana smiles.

Equally hurriedly, she returns to her apartment. When she opens the door she stops on the threshold. She is satisfied with what she sees. After a day's cleaning the apartment is as spotless and tidy as a hospital.

Everything is under control, she thinks. Just carry on as you are doing, calmly. First, drink a glass of wine. Then take your clothes off slowly and observe your naked body. Then make love to yourself and see how you do.

She carries out the first part of the plan – a glass of wine, a toast to herself, a slight tipsiness to coax her on – but the wine fails to do its job. She applies herself to the second part, but when she tries to make love to herself she feels nothing but embarrassment.

'You're pathetic,' she sneers. And goes to bed.

Before falling asleep, though, she swears to herself that the following Thursday, her day off, she will have a serious day of reckoning with her body. It's not enough just to touch yourself until you feel sore. She reaches the conclusion that she must study herself in the mirror. Deal with the sight of her flesh. Look at herself. She has a whole week to work on it. Otherwise why spend all that money on the mirror she hung in the corridor? She bought it in Ikea for thirty dollars. The hum of the air conditioning unit rubs her nerves raw. She tunes into it for a while and slides into sleep.

Seven days later she has an appointment with the mirror.

Let's take these rags off, she says to herself.

The hum of the air conditioning is still there, accompanied this time by the low rumble of the fridge. She turns the air conditioning unit off and closes the blinds. The building opposite is very close and there are no curtains on the windows.

She takes off her light-blue cotton t-shirt, but leaves her bra on. She takes her slippers off and places them carefully in a corner of the corridor, near the table with the phone on it. She takes her jeans off. The sky-blue panties she bought are a bit too big; at the next sales she'll buy some that fit better. Now she knows she needs extra small. She positions herself in front of the mirror.

She looks the other way and unclasps her bra. The air in the room is getting close. She closes her eyes and works her thumbs under the blue elastic. Her fingers meet over her flat stomach – every woman's dream, Lila says. She can feel a vein pulsing somewhere under her skin, to the left of her belly button. She keeps her eyes shut and shifts her hands downwards.

She slowly pulls down her panties, to her knees, to her ankles, folds them and puts them on the table. They are her last barrier of defense. She goes back to her original position and opens her eyes, being careful not to meet her own gaze.

She has no idea whether what she sees is beautiful or not. She's seen so few naked bodies in her life: Aunt

Katrina when she was already old, and Uncle Gjergj when he was dead and they had to prepare him for the wake. She can't remember ever seeing her mother in the nude.

She's happy that this time at least she's getting over her embarrassment. She feels better than she thought she would. She's spent so many years thinking about and fearing this moment and now it's just an ordinary instant of time, crudely banal, not at all special.

Stripping off in the freezing cold *kulla* and throwing water over yourself while standing in a copper washstand was not the same. For one thing there were no mirrors, and anyway she was Mark then. The rigors of mountain life crept into your most hidden thoughts. You did whatever the Doda family code of honor required you to do, and looking at your own naked body was simply wrong. That was the ancient code of the mountains. The Kanun inspired the greatest fear of all. It was as powerfully outlined and yet obscure as a recurring nightmare.

Hana tries to bring her attention back to her body. The man that she thought would still be tenaciously inhabiting her is no longer there. That man was only a carapace. Lila was right: Mark Doda's life had been no more than the sum total of the masculine gestures Hana had forced herself to imitate, in the skin worn leathery by bad food and lack of attention. Mark Doda had been a product of her iron will.

All that remains of that earlier existence are the sticking-out ribs and straight, shapeless legs she sees in the mirror. The breasts are no bigger than a young girl's. Hana feels her vulnerable optimism begin to crumble and she puts her clothes back on quickly before it's too late.

She goes into the tiny kitchen and makes herself a Turkish coffee. Lila has given her a *xhezve* coffeepot to brew it in. She watches the black liquid rise into a froth and takes it off the burner. She drinks it black, without sugar. She rinses out the cup. Then she calls Lila, who immediately asks her if anything's happened. Since Hana went to live on her own, Lila imagines disaster striking all the time.

'Nothing. I just wanted to say hi.'

'There's something else,' Lila insists.

'I looked at myself in the nude. I didn't look so bad.'

Hana can sense her cousin smiling at the other end of the line.

'I never doubted it,' Lila says. 'But there was no convincing you.'

'I think you need to help me with stuff like body cream and all that. My skin is really dry.'

Lila asks her if, by any chance, she's asking her to come over right away. Hana pauses. Then she confesses it would be great if Lila could sleep at her place, just tonight.

'I'm coming. I'll throw some clothes on and be right on over.'

'Thanks, Lila.'

They've turned the lights off. They both stare at the ceiling without saying a word. The bed is a queen size, not really big enough for two people, especially with one of them Lila's size. They bought it in a Salvation Army store. It creaks even when you don't shift your weight. Hana has christened it 'Jim.' In Albanian the word for 'bed' is masculine; in English things aren't masculine or feminine. So she calls this bed 'Jim.' Who knows whom he's arguing with to make such a racket. Maybe he remembers when he was still in the forest and couples used to lean on him to make love. He must miss the forest.

Hana enjoys giving names to things in the house. Not everything, just the big pieces of furniture. She started this game with Jonida, and her niece loved it.

Lying next to her, Lila smells of soap.

'How are you going to live like this, Hana?' she murmurs. 'All your life on your own?'

'Every now and then, you'll come. Like tonight. And then it'll be nice.'

'It's sad all the same.'

'No it isn't.'

'How come you never get angry? If I were in your position I'd go crazy.'

The veiled light of a lamppost and the distant roar of traffic cut through the silence. It's not a great area to live in. They say it's not safe. But Hana doesn't feel any danger when she goes out. And anyway, she can pay the rent here with the little she makes at the parking lot, and it's not far from Lila's.

'You didn't answer my question,' Lila pushes. 'How come you never get angry?'

'Who should I get angry with?'

'I don't know . . . ' Lila pauses as she rests her hands behind her head. 'With your crippled life.'

'Crippled? Well. I did feel angry, the first year after Uncle Gjergj died. But it wasn't really anger.'

They listen to the night.

'Have you ever been in love?' Lila asks her.

'Once. I think that's what it was. There was a boy. I could have loved him, but he left for France. He left before it turned into love.'

'Did he know you liked him? Did you ever tell him?'

'Kind of.'

'Kind of how?'

'We were in Albania, Lila.' Hana smiles up at the ceiling. 'You keep on forgetting.'

'Some things you forget, you're right.'

They stop talking for a while.

If you're a woman and you're Albanian, and you're from the mountains, and you're Catholic but your guilty-as-hell Christ was banned by the communists, then you don't have much choice but to try to suppress all those things they forced down your throat and had the gall to call life.

It wasn't life. It was the annihilating breath of fear. It was pain a whisper away from the atrocious pleasure of hearing death knock at the door, then move on. It was a daily ration of menace, a nightmare you couldn't escape.

In order not to go crazy, you try to forget, though of course you still carry the burden of your past under the cloak of everyday life. At that moment, in the middle of the night, it was sufficient to say, 'We were in Albania, Lila,' for it all to come rushing back.

'Tell me about the boy you liked.'

Hana tells her every detail, more than she has ever confessed, even to herself. She had written at least twenty poems dedicated to Arben Leska. They had helped her keep her head straight during the first few winters she had spent as a man, in between drinking raki and slapping the shoulders of the men of Rrnajë.

One day up there in the mountains a group of journalists had arrived to shoot a documentary. The communists had just left. Albania was in chaos. One of the foreigners – they were Italians – had donated a CD player, together with a few discs, to the village hut. There was a song about the Ten Commandments she had liked and she understood some of the words.

Honor your mother, honor your father, and honor his stick too.

She had honored what she had to honor. Now it was all over and she didn't want to ruminate over her pain forever.

'Shall we go to sleep?' Lila asks. Without waiting for an answer, she turns on her side and falls asleep, snoring gently.

The next morning it is raining just enough to wash away the defects of the roads and buildings around her. Lila has already gone, leaving behind a waft of cheap perfume.

Hana makes an effort to do something about her appearance. She's wearing the same pants, same shirt, same shoes. But she has two lipsticks. One is discreetly pink, the other a cherry red. This morning she chooses the bolder one and she's happy with her choice. As she goes out she looks back fondly at her apartment.

She climbs into her car and strokes the steering wheel before firing the engine. She loves Route 355. She knows every junction, every exit indicating a no through road. She even has a special feeling for the long sequence of traffic lights inviting her to pass, nearly always green for her. As she's driving she thinks back to the evening before in Lila's company.

It's not true that she wants to forget Rrnajë. It's not true at all. She may never find a man who's prepared to love her. She may never even receive a caress, even by mistake. She may be a parking-lot attendant until the day she dies. At the end of her life she'll probably speak excellent English. But somewhere in the middle, in the folds of all these maybes, sooner or later, she'll go back to the village for a last goodbye.

It's not a matter of settling accounts, or of having something to show off.

It's a matter of love for love's sake. She has a debt of love to Rrnajë. It's as simple as that. And that's how it will always be.

1996

Lila's letter arrives in Rrnajë one leaden-skied Wednesday. Hana finds it on the doorstep of her *kulla* at around ten in the morning. The postman didn't knock. He just left it there. Hana stares at the envelope for a long time without opening it. She runs her fingers over the American stamps. Then she puts the letter on the makeshift wooden table in the courtyard and goes inside for something to drink.

The *kulla* is cold. Spring is late this year, almost resentfully so, as if it had dragged itself up to the mountains against its will. Yesterday there was sunshine. It came suddenly and stayed nine hours. Hana counted them. The sun was brutally bright, shedding an indecent light on hidden aspects of the village. There's hunger written on the faces of all its inhabitants. Winter meals of beans and a few potatoes have made their eyes spectral. It's up to no good, that sun. It crept up on them so stealthily they hadn't had time to hide or disguise their suffering.

Hana looks at the photos of Gjergj and Katrina on the wall. She's proud of those two portraits. She had gone into the city to have them enlarged and framed. The photographer had said that it was much harder to do without the negatives and she would have to pay double. She had paid. She had a bit of money set aside. She was a truck driver and earned quite a good living. The agricultural cooperative where she had worked for years had closed. Now she grew her own vegetables. She had to adapt.

You're a good guy, Mark Doda would say to himself in a deep baritone when he was drunk. Mark liked getting drunk. He would float in an undefined dimension and be happy. As soon as he sobered up he would read over the poems he had scribbled while he had been drinking.

Hana wants to go outside, sit on the half-rotten chair in the courtyard and finally open Lila's letter. But she takes her time. She remembers that today some more foreigners are due in Rrnajë. The village has been waiting for them all week. At least there's something going on, something to help kill a bit of time.

When the foreigners arrive at the village, though, the few people still living there refuse to open their mouths. They sit in silence, proud and shy at the same time – although these days any real pride there was seems to have melted along with the snow in the sunshine. Even pride is hidden and fugitive. Westerners come and ransack stories from these 'primitive and mysterious' northern mountain folk. Anyone who wants to tell their life story can do so, and in return get foreign currency, dollars or Deutschmarks.

There are those who will blurt out any story that comes into their heads, who cares if it's true or not. Foreigners buy the stories they want to hear, and they don't care about the truth any more than the locals. In the old days it had been different. Mountain people were hospitable but hermetically sealed off from the world. They would open the doors to their *kullë*, but not to their inner world. You had to smell out their souls on your own, if you knew how. Now poverty has forced them to learn new tricks in a hurry, because pride doesn't put food on the table. Neither does work, for that matter; most of the year up in the mountains there is none.

Hana puts her hands to her head as if ready to unscrew and take it off. She feels a momentary flash of pleasure.

This winter there has been a lot of snow. She pines for previous winters when it mostly rained. The sound of dripping rain is company; rain doesn't isolate you as snow does. They're just little things, she thinks, nothing you can't get over. Little things.

She's disturbed by the name of the interpreter who's scheduled to arrive with the foreigners. She's called Blerta, like her best friend from college. She hasn't seen her since then. Why would she be coming up here with these foreigners?

She finally steps out into the courtyard. Don't get yourself worked up, she tells herself, while she observes her favorite hen, which she has called Angelina. Red from her beak to her tail feathers, she struts with a regal air. She's intelligent and a bit of a bitch. She steals pieces of bread from her companions when they aren't looking. But she's classy too. In a previous life she must have been someone famous, or a lion. Or perhaps the leader of a flock of migrating birds.

The sheep are nudging up to the table where Hana has put the dish of stale bread. The hens are beginning to worry they'll be trodden underfoot by the sheep, who start to butt at the table. She picks up the dish, walks over to the other side of the courtyard and scatters the food.

Lila writes:

Hey, Hana, dear cousin. Here I am, writing to you with so much nostalgia and admiration for what you are doing. People are talking, you know? They say you're a good truck driver, and that everyone respects you. The rumors come all the way here to America, you know? You'd better believe it. Some Albanians are here with a green card, and others are here on a three-month tourist visa to stay with relatives. You're the only one up there in cloud cuckoo land.

What are you doing there? I keep asking myself?
Why don't you come here? You'd be taking the most
important step in your life. You're wasting it, you
know? As if it wasn't your life to live. You should
think about it. Right, Hana? Do you promise, that
you'll think about it.

Her cousin has a problem with punctuation. What's a question mark doing after 'I keep asking myself'? And what about the comma after 'promise' in the last sentence? Sometimes Lila has a problem with logic too. There's only one thing she really does well, and that's make Hana cry, always. The other great thing about Lila is her love for Shtjefën. She loves him to bits. She calls him 'her harbor, her home, and her roof.' She's really something, Lila.

She goes and rinses her face in Aunt Katrina's copper washstand. Then she straightens up and casts a stern eye over the courtyard. It's time to get cracking, she tells herself. But the gleaming copper of the washstand catches her eye. She has never let it tarnish; she polishes it assiduously. It's the most beautiful object in the house. It was in Aunt Katrina's dowry chest. Before it became hers it had been her mother's and, before that, her grandmother's. Family tradition has it that it goes back two centuries. It is elegant and understated. The women of the house have only ever used it for washing their faces. One day, if she ever does make it to the United States, she'll take it with her. The thought courses through her like a bolt of lightning. Now it really is time to get cracking.

She mends the wooden fence that is falling apart. She cleans out the stable and gets the animals back in so that she can rake the whole courtyard clean. She checks on the seedlings she planted two weeks ago and covered with plastic sheeting. As she goes about all these chores she lights each cigarette from the one before.

If it doesn't rain, she'll finish all her jobs tomorrow. The day after tomorrow she'll deal with her Chinese truck. She needs to take it to Scutari to check the brakes. In the summer she uses it to transport vegetables into town and back, or to take people to weddings in Scutari or Lezhë.

Lila's letter has burrowed down into her guts. She goes over and over every passage in her mind: how Jonida is growing; how she and her husband are so beat after work they fall asleep on their feet; how well they feel and how they make ends meet even though there are still many hardships; how happy they would be to have Hana come stay with them.

> *This is the fourth time I've written you, Hana, and it's not easy for me to write so try and imagine how hard it is for me to put down all my thoughts in any kind of order and don't even think about giving me a hard time about it. So are you going to send me an answer? Do you want to come on vacation one time just to see what*

*it's like before making up your mind? You can't carry
on being a man just because once upon a time you had
to turn into one. If you wait too long you'll get old, and
old age is no picnic, they all say.*

When she hears knocking at the courtyard gate she's
covered in dirt and sweating. She shouts at the unknown
visitor to come in and waits with her hands thrust into
her pockets.

It's Blerta; Blerta's head peering shyly round the gate.
They look each other up and down. Hana imagines the
effect she's having on her old schoolmate, but decides not
to care. She pushes her hands deeper into her pockets.
Blerta is so womanly, so beautiful. Long, straight, very
blond hair, a long black V-neck sweater over a shirt and
red pants. Almost no makeup, just a hint of lipstick.

'Hey, Hana,' Blerta says.

'I'm Mark. I'm not Hana anymore, and you know it.'

'Yeah, of course I knew it, but I didn't know how to . . .'

'Cut it out.'

'Can I come in?'

'You're already in. Welcome, Blerta.'

Hana turns back towards the *kulla*, but she realizes
her friend isn't going anywhere. Hana stops in her tracks
without turning around.

'It's just you, I hope. You wouldn't bring your journalists, right?'

'No.'

'Ok then, come on in. I'm happy to have you here.'

Things are better inside the *kulla*. It's too dark inside for Blerta to keep on X-raying her. Hana feels more protected.

They sit down on the *shilte*. The guest looks around. Hana lights a cigarette and hands over the tin box where she keeps her rolling tobacco.

'No, thanks,' Blerta smiles guiltily. 'I don't smoke.'

'You smoked once, before the second exam.'

'Oh, yeah. You've reminded me . . . I'd forgotten that one . . .'

'Who are these foreigners? What are they doing up here?'

'They're English. They're making one of those documentaries on the Kanun code. I'm their interpreter, they pay well, and . . . '

'I heard you work in Tirana.'

'I did a master's for two years in the US, on a Fulbright scholarship. I came back six months ago and now I'm living in Tirana, yes.'

'Well well.'

Silence.

'I couldn't wait to meet you. You knew I would come, right?'

'Here everybody knows everything. There've been quite a few foreigners around recently.'

'I know.'

'What do you want from me, Blerta?'

'Nothing. I just came to see you.'

'No, you didn't come to see me. You came for your work and, as I'm the only enlightened man left in this God-forsaken village since all the real men were sacrificed to blood feuds or hunger, you thought you'd get me to help you.'

Blerta can't wait to get out. Hana enjoys watching her squirm. She takes one last puff of her cigarette and, before putting it out, lights the next.

Blerta has the courage to protest that Hana is being hostile and she doesn't understand why.

'Of course you don't understand. I have too much to do right now and I don't really want to talk.'

Blerta gets up. Hana admires her lithe body. She has shed all her provinciality.

'Anyway, we're staying here for three weeks,' Blerta says. 'I'm sorry I disturbed you.'

'Where are you sleeping?' Hana asks brusquely.

'In a *kulla*, in Theth.'

'And tonight?'

'In the same place. We're leaving in an hour.'

'You can sleep here if it doesn't disgust you.'

'No, I'd better be going. Take care of yourself, Hana.'

Blerta leaves. Hana puts a bottle of raki on the low table, and lays out some sheep's cheese and a can of olives she bought in Scutari a few weeks before. She drinks without stopping, even when the cheese and olives are finished. She drinks until the bottle is dry and passes out on the *kilim*.

For several days she doesn't show her face in the village. If she happened to bump into Blerta she wouldn't know how to behave. Fucking pride, she says to herself. She likes cursing. Let Blerta's hair go back to being frizzy! What a bitch, she thinks. You're a real bitch, Hana. You're still a woman with all that bitchiness inside you. You're no angel.

One day she leaves for Scutari. She still needs to check the brakes on the truck.

The mechanic is about forty-five and he loves his work. During the regime he had a factory job; now his kids have emigrated to Italy. Hana doesn't know which factory he used to work in. They all looked the same: old rusted ruins donated by Soviet Big Brother or Chinese Big Brother. It was as if, rather than machinery, they had housed iron carcasses held together with spit. The fact that her truck was made in China was a source of subtle pleasure, for the People's Republic was still under communism while insignificant little Albania had fought itself free. The mechanic's name was Farì.

'Freedom is all well and good, my friend,' he says to Hana. 'There's no doubt about it. But can you eat it? No.'

Hana watches his grease-covered hands as he gesticulates wildly. Hands look good when they're black like that, like coarse moths. If she were a photographer she would capture his hands on camera.

'I'll get this beast going for you,' Farì goes on, not waiting for her to answer. 'But first let's go and get ourselves some coffee.'

The café is crowded. The mechanic orders two espressos.

'Can I ask you something?' he says to Hana when the coffees are served. 'Why did you stay in Rrnajë? Why didn't you go abroad? You could have got a job in construction in Italy, Greece, France, or even America. Anywhere's better than here.'

Hana reminds him that he too has stayed behind in Albania. The mechanic shakes his head.

'My two boys left for Italy on the first ships out of here when the regime cracked. Now they're doing ok, but it was hard for them to start with. They went to a city called Treviso, in the north. They're pretty racist up there. If you say you're Albanian they think you're a criminal. Then they tried Greece and it was even worse. They went back to Italy, near Rome. They're both mechanics. Things got better there. Rome is a big city and they're hard workers, like me.'

Farì sits up straighter and smiles, revealing a missing tooth. Hana is missing two molars. She hasn't seen a dentist in seven years. She smiles back.

A muezzin starts his call. Scutari is full of mosques. Farì turns serious.

'When you have kids, you live for them, my friend,' he says. 'The old lady and me, we're staying here and we want to die here. Once we went to Rome to see the boys. They treated us like royalty.'

He makes an indecipherable gesture. He's a real father: pure paternal love exhibited without any hypocritical attempt to feign detachment.

'You, Mark, you should get away from this crazy country. You're still young. Can't you see the north of Albania is empty? They say there are over a million Albanians around the world who left as soon as this country became a democracy. And if you really don't want to leave the country, at least come down and live in the city. We could go into business together, what do you say? You could take care of the accounts, the clients, the spare parts to order down in Tirana. You've read a lot and you're good with paperwork, I hear. I've been thinking about it for a while, but I never had the chance to talk to you.'

Farì finishes his espresso with a hasty last gulp.

'Everyone with any education has gone. We dummies know how to work, but what about the mind? The mind, my friend – who has a mind around here any longer? You have brains enough and more. Think about it.'

'Thanks, Farì. I will.'

'Ok, let's get back to your Chinese heap of scrap.'

While Farì works on the truck, Hana smokes a cigarette, looking at her reflection in the filthy glass of the garage door. She looks like a scarecrow. Her cheeks are hollow, her hair matted, her shirt three sizes too big. The muezzin's still getting on their nerves with his whining.

Farì starts the truck. She moves away from the door and watches him as he drives by, vanishes around the corner, and takes the truck down a road that was once paved and is now a muddy track.

Thirty or forty years before, somewhere in the middle of that vast, faraway country, when the Chinese workmen had finished testing the truck destined for Albania that was already old before it even left the factory, the afternoon could have been just like this one.

Hana remembers the Chinese with their blue uniforms. She saw a group of five of them in Piazza Skanderbeg in Tirana, the first time she went there on a school trip. But they had also been on the television at the agricultural cooperative in Rrnajë. They were comical. People said they ate snakes; who knew if it was true. All they brought to Albania were broken-down trucks, bicycles without gears, a metalworks that was as old as the world itself and their dances with that boring, whiny music. The ones Hana remembers all looked sad. Maybe it was those instruments with their terrible twangy strings. Nothing like the north Albanian sword dance.

Farì is coming back in the truck, waving his left hand excitedly out of the window at her.

'You're all set here,' he says, proudly.

Hana thanks him, pays, and drives away.

A week later she goes to see Blerta. This time her friend's hair is tied back and she's wearing jeans and a white shirt. Two foreigners are filming in the center of the village. Blerta is standing behind them.

'I came to say hello,' Hana says, embarrassed. 'I wasn't very nice the other day, to put it mildly, so . . . '

'Don't worry. It's really lovely here. Is it always so peaceful?'

Wrong question, Hana thinks to herself. If only it were peaceful here.

'Are you married, Blerta?' she asks, rather than answering her friend's question. How did she get so beautiful? She used to be the kind of mousy girl you didn't notice; now she's a kind of goddess. Her eyes are the color of a stormy sea. She looks great in jeans. She would look good in a potato sack.

'No, I'm not married. I have a boyfriend, though. He lives far away, in the US.'

Hana looks at her inquisitively.

'We lived together for a while but then he didn't want us to get married. He felt it was too soon, he didn't feel ready. So here I am.'

'Do you ever speak to this friend?'

'He calls every week.'

'So it's serious.'

'I don't really know, but he goes on calling.'

Hana tells Blerta she has come to invite her to dinner.

Two old women shuffle by, pushing barrows loaded with potatoes and sacks of flour. All the menfolk in the clan of one of the women live permanently locked inside their *kulla*, under the threat of an ancient blood feud. Only she can leave the house without risk of being shot and killed. The Kanun says that women, children, and priests are not targets. The old woman's clan is in a blood feud with a clan from Bogë. Before moving away, Hakia – that is her name – catches Hana's eye. She doesn't say hello, but a corner of her mouth lifts in a light grimace, hinting at a greeting. Hakia's eyes are a tree waiting for the ax to fall. What must it be like to live with ten men shut up in your *kulla*, the only thread of hope for so much frustrated virility? The history of blood spilled between the two families goes back a hundred years, relieved only by a brief truce imposed by the communists. Hakia had a hundred years of death in her memories.

Hana shifts her attention to Blerta and asks her what she studied in the US.

'Psychology and psychiatry in Seattle, a city in the state of Washington, in the northwest.'

'I don't know anything about all that,' Hana smiles. 'So, are you coming over this evening?'

'As soon as I'm done with these journalists. Is around eight ok?'

Hana cuts some cheese and arranges it as best she can on the only good serving dish in the house. It's an old porcelain plate from Turkey; Aunt Katrina held onto it like a relic. Hana mashes the beans she boiled that morning and makes a kind of purée. She fries up a few onions and aromatic herbs and mixes them into the purée. As she doesn't have a suitable bowl to serve it in, she puts everything into a saucepan and shreds a few hot chili peppers over the top.

The next step is a painstaking wash. She combs her wet hair back. If she had a bit of face cream she would put it on. She puts on her best flannel shirt, bought in Lezhë market. What the hell? She stops and asks herself. What do you think you're doing?

Just then Blerta looks round the door.

'Hey, Hana! Can I give you a hug this time?' she asks as soon as she's inside, not wasting a moment.

'Let's hug then, if it means so much to you.'

They embrace for a few, embarrassed seconds. Blerta doesn't seem to want to let go, so Hana focuses on the picture of Gjergj in front of her, or rather, on his left mustache, curled up and black as pitch.

'Look, Blerta. I'm a man, you know.'

'Ok. You're a man and I'm the big bad wolf.'

'Leave off now.' Hana detaches herself and darts over

to the table, where she starts fiddling with the aluminum forks, lining them up. Blerta sits down.

'Hana,' she says sweetly. 'Relax! I'm Blerta, your old friend from college, and I came to see you, ok?'

'There's some bean purée and sheep's cheese for dinner, with black bread and as much raki as you like, if you want to get drunk.'

'I don't drink raki,' Blerta says, apologetically.

But Hana pours some out anyway and Blerta doesn't stop her. They eat the bean dish with the cheese, and it's delicious.

They talk about this and that, in a desultory way. Then Blerta says that sooner or later she'd like to have a child – if not with the American then with someone else. Anything's possible these days, right?

Hana proposes a toast. They lift their glasses and drink to it. Blerta screws up her face while Hana tosses the raki back as if it were water, fills their glasses up again, and watches in amazement as Blerta takes another gulp. Now they're both beginning to relax.

'I know you're annoyed with me because I didn't come up to the mountains to visit after you took your oath.'

'We're not talking about that.'

'Yes we are. We need to because it's been bothering me ever since, and we talked about my visiting you for months in college.'

'Then you forgot all about me,' Hana says, without rancor.

Blerta reaches for the bottle of raki, slips her shoes off and makes herself more comfortable. Now Hana recognizes the old Blerta from ten years ago, sitting cross-legged on the bunk bed at Tirana University students' residence. She had been funny and shy and secretly in love with all the boys who walked under their window. Hana had dedicated a poem to Blerta but hadn't been able to give it to her because of Aunt Katrina's death.

'Yes. For years I hoped you would come up and see me at least once,' she confesses. 'I mean, in those early years, why didn't you come?'

Blerta struggles not to let the alcohol confuse her, but she goes on drinking.

'Would it have changed anything?' she asks, rubbing her eyes. 'These beans are delicious, by the way.'

'No, it wouldn't have changed anything.'

Hana doesn't want this evening to vanish into thin air. She doesn't want Blerta to disappear again, she doesn't want to go back to being Mark, nor for her life to slip by without the chance to understand something about herself.

'You look like a foreigner, and you make me ashamed of myself.'

'Foreign? Me?' Blerta objects.

'The way you move, your perfect English . . . I heard you this afternoon talking to those people in your group.

You know how much I love that language and how I never got to study it properly. You make me feel ugly and stupid. What can I say?'

Her friend smiles at her.

'You were beautiful once, but you did your best not to let anyone see it.'

'Me?'

'Yes, you. With all those guys chasing after you!'

'Chasing after me?' she asks, because she likes hearing the words. You're enjoying this, she says to herself. What an idiot. What a stupid idiot.

'You're still beautiful now, you know?' Blerta says, her voice suddenly turning sad. 'Despite your best efforts to destroy your looks.'

'Don't say that.'

Blerta says she has to say these things, because now she can see with her own eyes that what everyone said was true.

Hana swallows the last two spoonfuls of beans and washes them down with alcohol. She gets up and opens the narrow window. What she'd really like to do is talk about books with Blerta, to go and get her notebooks full of poems and throw them into her friend's lap so she could laugh at Hana as much as she wanted.

She rests her forehead on the stone wall.

'Thanks for being here today, Blerta,' she says.

'All these years, I never really believed you were gay or that you had become a man in order to hide that you were.'

'Is that what people said?'

'Well, you didn't tell us what was going on. You didn't send a card or anything, an invitation to come see you. So we left you in peace. That's why we didn't get in touch.'

Hana comes back and sits down with her legs crossed. She tries to see herself through Blerta's eyes. I must look like a tiny version of Gjergj Doda, she thinks. But that's not what Blerta sees. She has never seen Hana's uncle, except in the photo on the wall.

'It can't have been easy,' her friend muses, her voice thick with drink, 'to live this way.'

Hana licks her finger and uses it to gather up the breadcrumbs on the table and stick them in her mouth. She looks up.

'It has been hard,' she answers, smiling. 'No, I correct myself, it's been hell.'

She had never thought about it in these terms before. She stiffens, now, in sudden anticipation of the inevitable question: 'Why did you do it?' Sooner or later that question always comes up and she doesn't want to hear it. Blerta surprises her by not saying anything. She's so quiet that Hana is almost angry with her. Her friend tells her she doesn't want any explanations about her choices because there wouldn't be any point. What's done is done.

Blerta is still the best. Hana laughs, conscious of her yellow teeth, dry skin and matted hair. Tears start to fall down her face and she does nothing to stop them. Blerta is crying too. Maybe it's the raki she can't take, or she's missing her American friend. Hana doesn't look at her. She listens to her sobs and feels almost relieved. She dries her cheeks and waits for Blerta's sadness to lose its edge.

Her friend sniffs loudly. In a few days she'll leave Rrnajë just as she came, and they may never see each other again. The idea of never seeing Blerta again gives Hana a spike of pain.

'Tell me about those years, Hana, if you feel like it? Tell me what it has been like, what it is like now.'

'There's nothing to tell.'

'Ten years of your life and there's nothing to tell?'

'No.'

'I don't believe you.'

'I don't give a damn.'

'About what?'

'About you not believing me.'

'Come on, I beg you.'

Hana laughs, her tears gushing again while she desperately tries to shame her heart into indifference.

'You can't talk about your own death. Find me a dead body that has succeeded and I'll take my hat off to it.'

Blerta thinks about this for a while and then tries to get her friend laughing again. 'You're the same old drama queen, I see.'

'I wish! I'm just pathetic, that's all.'

They both laugh.

They stretch out on the *shilte*, each absorbed in their own thoughts.

There's nothing to tell. Blerta will go off, and Hana will go back to being Mark again. There are some advantages to being a man. You do very little. The women do all the real work. Especially when there's snow, men lie around doing sweet nothing. They give orders, they drink, they clean their rifles. Or they use them. There have been a lot of shooting deaths since freedom came to Albania.

The law in the north dictates that men have to take care of the family land, money, rifles, and honor. Now people want their land back, but when the communists expropriated it they did away with all the land deeds. The result is that nobody knows who legitimately owns what. In order to make things clearer, men in these parts often use their rifles. Hundreds of deaths and hundreds of women dressed in mourning. So many children left fatherless.

'So what are your plans?' Blerta asks, stretching out her legs. 'Are you planning to go on being a man?'

I forgot to smoke, Hana thinks to herself. That's incredible. The tobacco isn't even on the table.

She gets up, finds the tin box with the two-headed eagle on it, sits down, and takes out the tobacco.

'I don't know,' she answers, without looking up. 'It's not like one day you become a man, then another you decide to become a tiger or a giraffe.'

'I know the rules. I studied the Kanun too – I know you're stuck. That's why I'm asking you.'

'What's done is done,' Hana says. She smiles as she rolls her cigarette. 'What's done can't be undone.'

'You should get away from here.'

'Don't start that. You sound like my cousin Lila. Do you remember her? She's living in the US now.'

'Really?' Blerta exclaims, sadness creeping into her expression. As soon as anyone mentions America she falls into a deep well of unhappiness: her American boyfriend, the unfulfilled dream of a baby.

Hana tells Blerta about Lila and the atmosphere eases again. Blerta laughs and so does Hana. In an alcohol-induced state of grace, they tell each other jokes and trade gossip about their old college acquaintances. Blerta talks about where so-and-so ended up, who married whom, which foreign city – Berlin, Perth, Delhi, Quito, Amsterdam, Alaska – they had emigrated to. Albanians left their country to conquer the world without warships, with no colonial language to force onto distant populations, no credit cards, no return fare.

'It's just the two of us,' Blerta concludes. 'And sooner or later we'll leave too. Maybe.'

They fall asleep on the floor.

They don't see each other for another four days. This time Hana wrings the neck of one of her hens for dinner in Blerta's honor, and grills it out in the open, in her courtyard. She boils some potatoes too.

Her friend arrives looking exhausted but happy. She has brought a bottle of Merlot from Scutari. Hana tells her there are no good knives in her *kulla* so she's not sure how to deal with the chicken. Blerta pulls at it with her hands, the meat coming off the bone easily. It is perfectly cooked.

'Is it because of the American that today you're in a good mood?' Hana asks her.

'He called last night. He's coming to Tirana. Can you believe it? Next week. How did you guess?'

Hana laughs. She takes the potatoes out of the clean cloth she wrapped them in to keep warm. They put all the food on the table and Blerta uncorks the bottle of Merlot.

'I can't believe he's really coming. I hardly dare believe anything.'

'Nobody comes to this shit-hole of a country for some stupid love affair. This time he must have thought about things a little more deeply.'

'Don't say anything. Once bitten, twice shy!'

They sit with their glasses filled.

'So here's to your health . . . to the man of the house!' Blerta toasts.

Hana pokes her nose into the glass and sniffs the scent of the wine. She looks at her friend.

'What's sex like?' she asks, point blank.

Blerta, who has her glass held up at eye level, lowers it so that she can look at Hana.

'You've lived with a man. Tell me, what's it like?'

Blerta tries to focus on the question, but she can't find a good answer and tells Hana the question is too big.

'Just tell me what it's like,' Hana insists. 'I mean, on a range from nothing special to the traditional disappointment of Albanian women, and then to the newfound sexual freedom in the cities, how important is sex in everyday life? For someone like you, Blerta, for example. How important is it?'

Blerta takes a sip of her wine.

'Sex is great. In my experience it's great,' she says, perfectly naturally.

'So it's worth trying, huh?'

'Yes, Hana, it's worth trying.'

'Great!' Hana sighs.

DECEMBER 2002

On the pinboard hanging in the kitchen, muddled in with shopping lists and to-do lists, there is a small piece of paper with a reminder written on it: 'Call Patrick O'Connor!' It has been there for months, the color fading over time.

Hana wrote it, that's for sure, but the idea seemed crazy so she never called. She only allows herself to do sensible things, and calling O'Connor is not sensible. But she still thinks about it. She's thought about it quite a lot. Especially since Lila started casually introducing her first to a colleague, then to a friend of Shtjefën's, then again to a distant relative of Pal's who lives in Ohio. After these clumsy attempts at matchmaking, Hana threatened to cut Lila out of her life if she didn't back off and stop playing the go-between. She didn't come all the way to the US to end up married to some Good Samaritan. Lila was upset, but she got the message and stopped.

In the early days, thinking about O'Connor had upset her, but these days it doesn't. She wants to meet someone who understands what she has been through, and until now she hasn't met a man she feels at ease with. Anyway, she enjoys thinking about him. She remembers his hands. She remembers his smell when they sat together on the Zurich–Washington flight. In a fleeting moment of total sincerity she even admits that maybe she dares to think about him precisely because he's unreachable. Never mind. It's just a series of maybes. That's the point. Maybe she hasn't forgotten him because there's no one else to remember. Maybe the solitude of this past year has been so good for her that it has cleared the way for her to think about the unattainable.

This December day, however, everything seems possible. She's succeeded in getting a job as a salesperson in a big, prestigious bookstore. If that's possible, all the rest is possible, reasonable even – including making a phone call to Patrick O'Connor. She'll be working in the bookstore for three months, on a maternity leave substitution. Then it's up in the air.

Jonida has come over to Hana's place to give her a face scrub. Before getting started she puts Coldplay on at full volume and tells her aunt they're her favorite group and that if she doesn't think they're the best she'll have to learn to like them.

While Jonida puts an exfoliating gel on Hana's face, Hana thinks back over the events of the last few weeks.

The most important, of course, was getting her new job. And it wasn't even that difficult. She saw the ad on the door of the bookstore and called Jonida straight away to tell her about it. As if it were a matter of national interest, Jonida dictated her strategy: Hana was to go in right away and ask for the manager before they hired someone else. Hana protested that they might already have found someone.

'They would have taken the notice off the door, duh!' Jonida teased. 'Or are you scared of trying? Don't tell me you're pissing yourself . . . '

Hana had put down the phone and gone into the bookstore. Two hours later she was hired. The wages weren't great but she had a thirty percent discount on all the books. She thanked the manager with tears in her eyes.

Lila gave her an earful about leaving the security of the parking lot. But then she relented and conveyed her best wishes along with the gift of a new linen pants suit.

Hana is due to start work immediately after the winter break, on January 2. Jonida is staying over for the weekend, deeply committed in her improvised role as Hana's beautician.

'How about changing the music?' Hana asks timidly.

Her niece looks daggers at her. 'Oh come on! You're not saying you're not into Coldplay?'

'Not really.'

'You totally don't understand a thing.'

'Ok, ok, but don't you have anything softer?'

'Well, just by chance I have some U2 here. You'll like them 'cause they're, like, old.'

Jonida wipes away the gel and spreads a thick layer of hydrating face mask over Hana's face. She goes and changes the track and warns Hana they will also need a makeup and cosmetics session. Hana protests.

'I'm not asking your permission,' Jonida ripostes. 'You've been here for, like, more than a year, and your whole life a man has never been near you. Now you have this great job, and contact with the public, you'll totally meet new people. So . . . '

Hana stretches. She's put on a few pounds, making her rounder and more feminine. Her hair has grown down to her shoulders; it's well cut and she looks gamine.

'I don't have a man, but I do have a working computer,' Hana argues. 'And I have some male friends I sometimes go out and have a drink with after work.'

'Yeah, right. Like Jack at the parking lot!' Jonida laughs.

'Of course.'

'But he's such a douche, and he has so many problems.'

Hana takes her niece's comments badly. 'I don't care if Jack's a douche or if he has problems. He's a dad, with two little kids and an alcoholic ex-wife. So what? He's a good person. He's straightforward and grounded.'

'Sorry,' Jonida apologizes. 'I didn't mean to offend anyone.'

'You're so cynical, you young people. Can you get this stuff off my face?'

U2 ricochet around the room with a song called 'Sunday Bloody Sunday.' Jonida takes a cotton-wool pad and wipes the excess cream from Hana's face. She suddenly turns serious. She wants to say something but gives up, scratches her chin and puts the dirty pad down on the kitchen table.

'My words came out all wrong,' she says, going over to the washbasin. She apologizes again. 'It's because I'm worried about you. After a whole year you know nothing about all that stuff. I mean . . . '

Hana opens the fridge and takes out a carton of juice.

'You don't seem to understand that I'm in no hurry.'

'Jeez, Hana, you're so boring! You're always saying the same thing.'

'And you'll hear me saying it again and again, until you guys learn not to stress me out.'

'What do you mean "you guys"?'

'I mean you and your mother – she's also trying to push me. You know she even tried to find me a boyfriend?'

Jonida gets edgy.

'I'm not my mom, if you haven't noticed.'

Hana goes up to Jonida and hugs her. Jonida holds back a little.

'Don't get angry, please, I beg you,' Hana whispers in her ear. 'You're smart and really mature for your age, but you can't understand everything. I can't run before I can walk.'

They break their embrace.

'Why do we always have to talk about me around here? Don't we have anything better to do?'

'Honestly? You still look a bit scared. And time is going by, Hana.'

Jonida is wearing a pair of military-style fatigues with big outside pockets, and a zippered cardigan. Her hair cascading around her face makes her look at least two years older than she is. Hana takes a quick look at the time: it's seven o'clock.

'Let's go out! What do you say?' Hana proposes. 'Let's forget all this stuff. We're just going around in circles. I'll take you to Georgetown.'

'You really go for those rich-guy hangouts, huh?' Jonida jokes as she goes to freshen up.

'I sure do!' Hana exclaims. 'And I'm ready to take you there. We'll take Route 355 all the way.'

Jonida complains that Route 355 is the slow route. The highway would be much faster.

Hana decides to take Route 355 anyway. She's done the last section three or four times on her own now, so that one day she'll be confident enough to take someone else. The Capital Beltway still makes her nervous.

Jonida hums a tune in the car. In ten days it will be Christmas. In eighteen days, Hana is starting her new job in the bookstore. Her niece taps her on the shoulder and smiles her most irresistible smile; she leans over and rests her head on Hana's shoulder. Going into ninth grade has made her grow up quickly. Soon she won't be looking for cuddles, Hana thinks, and then it'll be like a desert, a new ice age, death. But Jonida has not left for college yet, she thinks, so stop being so masochistic.

'You're thinking I'm growing up fast, right?' Jonida guesses. 'You have the same look as Mom when she starts saying she won't be able to live without me when I go to college.'

Hana laughs. So all mothers are the same, she thinks. She feels maternal towards Jonida, but she tries not to make it too obvious so that Lila doesn't feel like Hana's trying to muscle in on her exclusive relationship with her daughter.

She finds a parking spot on P Street. While they are walking into the center of Georgetown, Jonida starts chattering about school, her friends, her geometry teacher who's totally cool and gets the students interested in the subject, her high grades in American history.

When they sit down at a table near the window in a snug little Vietnamese restaurant, Hana is filled with a sense of overpowering happiness.

The next day she takes Jonida back home. Lila and Shtjefën offer her a cup of coffee and they start discussing what to cook for Christmas Day. Lila is on a diet and has started going back to the dentist to work on her teeth and improve her smile. Every now and then she goes to the hairdresser and straightens her long, curly hair. Shtjefën explains that his wife is trying to keep him interested, otherwise his virile good looks might end up attracting some other woman. Lila smiles.

'What do you expect? Apart from Jonida I only have you. And every day she's getting further away, however much love we give her.'

She sighs and looks at Hana.

'Are we doing something wrong with this girl?' she asks Hana in a whisper. Jonida has vanished into her room. 'How was she yesterday? She goes over to your place as soon as she gets the chance. It feels like she's trying to get away from us.'

'Oh come on, baby,' Shtjefën chips in. 'You go to Hana's all the time too, like tomorrow, for instance. Does that mean you're trying to get away from Jonida and me?'

When she gets back to her apartment, Hana puts on a pair of baggy red sweatpants and checks the to-do list on her board. At the top of the list there's an exhortation to read the computer manual and practice doing some Google searches.

She sips a cup of tea as she reads the manual attentively. She feels as though she's understanding everything, and she's proud of herself. But rather than starting to surf the Web straight away, she sits there, completely immobile, suddenly unsure where the evening is taking her. For sure, she has made some huge steps. She's completely self-sufficient in all her daily activities and needs no help at all. She pays her bills online. She can speak fairly fluently, and she can read Emily Dickinson, Sylvia Plath, Gloria Naylor, and Toni Morrison, as well as an army of male poets and writers. She has pages and pages of notes on English idioms and phrases spread all over the house; her fridge is like a school whiteboard.

'But between my legs, things are still pretty dry,' she says out loud. She stares at the empty teacup. It's her favorite, the color of a green lawn. She calls it Melissa. She likes the name Melissa.

She thinks the time has finally come for her to lie down close to a man and smell his body, even though she keeps telling Lila and Jonida she's in no hurry. In her diary she has written: 'Hana desires a man.' Then she added an exclamation mark. But she can't confide in anyone about these things. Not Jonida, and certainly not Jack.

She saw a program on TV where women were saying they solved the problem by using a vibrator. But she has no idea where she could buy one. She tells herself she's pathetic thinking about all this filth, and tries to focus on the computer. But all her attempts to get started go nowhere. Sex is on her brain today and she can't stop thinking about it.

The next evening Lila comes to Hana's house with some *byrek* pastry she has made at home and wrapped in a damp cloth. She walks into the kitchen without even saying hello and asks Hana if the oven is already on.

Hana leans on the door frame and doesn't move. Lila turns around.

'What are you doing there? Hurry up! The pastry has risen and it can't wait. Shtjefën's coming at nine.'

Lila dusts the kitchen table with flour. Hana, still standing, asks her if she has ever made love to herself and if she happens to have a vibrator. Lila opens and shuts the kitchen drawers, apparently looking for a rolling pin.

'Answer my question.'

'A vibrator.'

'That's what I said.'

'We have sex in the normal way with the tools God gave us. What kind of question is that anyway?'

'Why are you going red?'

'Where do you keep your rolling pin?'

Hana takes it out of the bottom drawer and hands it to Lila.

'Don't get so anxious. I asked if you had a vibrator, not a Kalashnikov.'

'Ok, ok. Yes, we have one. We got hold of one as a kind of joke. Jeez, I can't believe we're even having this conversation.'

Hana lets Lila roll out the pastry, taking her time, while she warms up the meat sauce and dices the mozzarella.

'I want to buy myself a vibrator,' she announces as she greases the baking pan.

'For crying out loud, can we change the subject here? Isn't there a radio or something in this house?' Lila layers pastry, meat sauce and cheese, drizzling olive oil over each layer and seasoning the *byrek* with pepper and oregano.

'I don't see why you're so bothered,' Hana insists.

Lila opens the oven door, pulling away as the rush of hot air hits her. She puts the baking tray in and closes the door. Hana sits down. Lila stays standing, suddenly awkward.

'You're always complaining I don't talk, and now you're making things difficult for me.'

'We're Albanians, Hana. We don't talk about these intimate things.'

'Well if you don't talk about them then you shouldn't do them either.'

'Well I don't. It's Shtjefën who likes trying things out. He says we need to be a little westernized or what's the point of being here? Not just to work our asses off. What would you do with those things anyway? You don't even have a man.'

'Exactly. I don't even have a man.' Hana's mood darkens. 'How come you don't understand?'

She goes and gets the wine she has already uncorked so it could breathe. She takes out two glasses and pours one for herself. She takes a sip. Lila wipes the kitchen table clean and pours herself a glass, but doesn't drink.

'I'm thirty-five years old now,' Hana explains in a whisper. 'Can you imagine being with a man for the first time and asking him to go easy because I'm a virgin? At my age? I'd be a joke. I don't even dare think about it. I can't imagine moving on from being just friends to being intimate. And that's why I never even try.'

There's a moment of pure embarrassment.

'I can't seem to make love to myself,' Hana goes on. 'I'm getting desperate. I feel like I'm sick or something. I thought things would be easier.'

Lila's tender gaze is directed somewhere behind Hana.

'Of course you can't make love on your own. You've never reached orgasm, Hana. Usually a woman learns to get pleasure from masturbation after she has had full sex. You need a man to find out what you really feel, to see whether you feel pleasure. You can't lose your virginity on your own, if that's your crazy idea when you ask me for a vibrator.'

Hana drops her head on the table. 'I'm in deep shit.'

'You knew that,' her cousin reminds her, without any reproach.

'I feel like shit too.'

Lila gets up and slowly tidies the kitchen. When she senses Hana has calmed down a little, she sits next to her.

'The first man you make love to, or have sex with, will have to be a very special man. Or else, you can find a guy just to help you get over your problem with your virginity. In any case he'll need to be gentle and sensitive.'

Hana looks up at her cousin.

'Eureka! What a discovery!' Hana exclaims, forcing a smile. 'And where am I going to find one of those? On Mars?'

'What's your problem all of a sudden?' Lila asks. 'You've taken it easy up to now. You wasted more time on your damn books than on yourself. You got pissed at me because I was hurrying you, and now you're panicking and being totally negative.'

Hana stands up.

'Don't worry about it. I'll get over it.'

She starts taking the knives and forks out of the dresser drawer and Lila gets up to help her. They work well as a team; they complement each other and neither gets in the other's way in the narrow kitchen.

'Things'll be fine. As soon as I start my new job I'll be fine.'

'A new job is not going to work miracles, my dear cousin.'

Hana doesn't argue with her and for a while they sit in silence. Lila switches on the TV and zaps through several channels without finding anything she wants to watch. Hana only has the basic package on her cable: twenty-one dollars a month for thirty channels without HBO or quality movie channels. Lila ends up on a channel showing a documentary about some 9/11 survivors.

Hana checks the *byrek* in the oven, following the images on the screen out of the corner of her eye.

In the village square, that day back in Rrnajë, they had kept firing their rifles all night to celebrate Frrok's daughter's engagement. The men had dragged the chairs from the café tavern out onto the square and grabbed a few bottles of raki as they went. The women wore their party dresses. They had looked beautiful, with the colored headscarves of their folk costumes sewn with coins in a fringe over their foreheads chinking in joyous cacophony. Hana had felt her stomach clench painfully.

Men and women were never together at parties and funerals. Hana had to stick with the men. That was the rule of the Kanun. Watching the women dance with the children that afternoon, the younger men had murmured their appreciation, discreetly, without going overboard or being vulgar. Then the evening turned cold, and the men dragged the chairs back inside together with the raki bottles.

The old television set had failed to work for a while. The silent images beamed across the screen with frequent interruptions. The color faded into black and white then came back again.

When the airplane hit the skyscraper, Tonìn Palushi had said that the big wide world out there was in as much trouble as they were. 'Just look at what pops into some people's heads, flying through a skyscraper to get from one side to the other.'

The pilots must be drunk, some men commented. That must be why they got confused. With all that sky above their heads to fly in, did they have to land right there in the building?

They had gone on drinking. Lul, who worked at the tavern, slammed his hand down on the television set a couple of times to try and get the sound back, but to no effect. The men cursed. Lul started frying cheese and the sizzling oil was the only sound to accompany the images.

Hana had wondered what Lila was doing at that precise moment in America, and whether the towers were in the city where she lived. Tonìn Palushi had added that the two pilots must be friends. They had to be. The other men nodded their agreement. Lul served the fried cheese, bread, and more raki. If the Americans did these things they must have good reasons, Bessian from the Shala clan concluded.

'Here's to the health of Frrok and his daughter. The Americans know what they're doing. It's not for us to worry about them.'

Hana remembers that, if she had been able, she would have crashed into the women's room in the *kulla* that afternoon just as the airplanes had crashed into the towers. She would have rushed in without asking permission and with all the men staring after her in shock. She would have defied all the rules, rebelled against their power. And, together with the women, she would have burst into tears.

Hana takes the *byrek* out of the oven and rests the baking tray on a cork mat. Lila hesitates, looks at Hana, and then launches into her speech.

'I have an idea, and I'll tell you what it is, though you may find it really dumb.'

The heat of the oven caresses Hana's left cheek.

'You can get rid of your virginity by going to see a gynecologist. I can take you to mine.'

Hana smiles and strokes her cheek.

'You don't need to tell her your life story. You can just explain that you want to make sure everything is ok for your first time. She'll understand fine without need-ing to hear all the details. It's easy for her to do it. It's a simple, technical procedure and it could make things easier for you.'

They're unable to discuss it further because Shtjefën arrives.

Eight days later Hana decides to go to the gynecolo-gist on her own. The doctor treats Hana with respect and professionalism. She doesn't know what Lila told the doctor – she doesn't really want to know. When she's done she pays in cash and steps out of the doctor's office feeling relieved, with the doctor's 'Good luck' resounding in her ears.

At home Lila is waiting anxiously.

'Thank you,' Hana says. 'I should have thought of it sooner. I feel much better.'

'Good,' Lila says, back to her usual practical tone. 'Now you just need to find a man.'

2003, SUMMER, AUTUMN

Work at the bookstore is relentless. Hana wants coffee and something sweet. She didn't have breakfast this morning and she feels a little dizzy. Lucky it's nearly the end of her shift and she'll soon be able to go home and get some sleep. Forget evening reading.

She looks up to call the next customer in line and finds Patrick O'Connor, holding three books and a political journal. He hands them to Hana with a distracted 'Good evening,' but when their eyes meet he focuses on her, and then looks totally confused.

'Good evening.' Hana smiles, trying to sound as normal as possible. 'Do you have a loyalty card, Mr O'Connor?'

Now he recognizes her. Still more confused, the shy smile he tries out on her rapidly fades. He pulls out his loyalty card and passes it to Hana, who slides it through the electronic reader.

'I'm Mark Doda. You're not wrong there. It's not a mistake.'

He mumbles something inaudible.

'I did tell you on the phone that you would find me different,' she says, trying to hand him a lifeline.

The man fiddles with his wallet, and Hana feels emotion paralyzing her. But she goes on smiling.

'I didn't think you'd be *this* different,' O'Connor manages to say. 'You were . . . er . . . pretty vague on the phone.'

'It wasn't easy to tell you the whole story on the phone. I couldn't face it. I apologize.'

O'Connor adjusts the lapels of his jacket for no reason.

'Look, I'm sorry. I didn't want to embarrass you.'

'Anyway, I recognized you right away,' he quips, trying to rescue them from this awkward moment.

Hana looks past him. The line of customers waiting to pay is getting longer; the cash registers are all working. She hands over the bag holding his books. O'Connor's eyes are deep blue, his forehead is high. He must be in his fifties. Light-skinned and physically fit.

'I don't usually come to this neighborhood,' he goes on, taking control. Hana is already regretting that she called him. 'I had a doctor's appointment nearby and had some time to spare, so here I am.'

'I don't know why I called you, but what's done is

done, right?' she says, squirming with embarrassment as she realizes her cheeks are burning bright red. She looks again at the customers in line.

'Before we go on, what am I supposed to call you?' O'Connor asks. 'And if I'm not being indiscreet, what time do you get out of here?'

'Hana. Call me Hana. My last name is the same. My real name has always been Hana Doda.' She enunciates it clearly, and he nods that he understands. 'It's my given name. In northern Albanian it means "moon."'

'Ok, Miss Moon,' O'Connor says, smiling, finally more at ease. 'I'd like to wait for you, or see you at some other time, if that is to your liking.'

'Look, you don't have to do this, you know.'

'I know I don't have to. But if you'll allow me, at this point I'm curious. Dead curious.'

Hana finishes her shift in twenty minutes and he says he'll wait at the bookstore café. He leaves, with a nod of his head and a smile. He walks with a stride, his shoulders straight, like someone accustomed to hiding their fears. Or maybe he has none, because life has always treated him well. And she has made a giant mistake when she didn't hang up as soon as she heard him in person on the other end of the line rather than the voice mail she had got the other times she tried. You've made this mess, now deal with it, she says to herself, calling the next customer in line to come and pay.

Half an hour later, when she sits in front of him, he smiles at her. He's had time to think about this unexpected meeting, she thinks. He's also had time to finish an espresso and flip through the newspaper. He crosses his arms and leans back on his chair. Hana experiments with a smile, shrugging her shoulders, and tries to hold his gaze. He's in no hurry to start the conversation.

Before coming over and sitting down, Hana has spent a little time in the ladies' room. She powdered her cheeks lightly. No bags under her eyes; last night she slept well. Lucky she decided to wear the jeans that fit her properly. Being androgynous has its advantages, she tells herself. She won't be good-looking whatever she does and, anyway, she's not here to please him – she lies – she's here to put herself to the test. She's still lying. She would like to make a dazzling impression. She would like to look enigmatic and translucent and deep and unusual and rare. She's just tiny, plain and cheaply dressed, with a guy who is clearly sophisticated sitting opposite her.

'Listen,' she says, beginning the conversation herself since there seemed to be no alternative. 'Go easy on me, and stop staring at me like that.'

He goes on stripping off her skin with his eyes, layer after layer. Only now he's doing it more delicately, trying not to look over-curious.

'I'm sorry,' he says. 'It's just I don't really know how I'm supposed to behave.'

'It's not easy for me either.'

'Right then, shall we make things a bit easier for ourselves?'

'Ok,' she decides. 'Me first, since I'm the one who dragged you into this situation. I'm a woman. I've always been one. I'm not a transvestite, or a transsexual, and I'm not gay. I've never been any of these things. It's just that I swore to become a man, in a social sense, sixteen years ago. I had to do it because my circumstances forced me to. The Kanun, the collected laws and traditions of northern Albania, allows a woman to become a man and give up her female role forever if she wants to, or if the head of the family orders her to. So I'm what they call a "sworn virgin." You've researched the Balkans and Albania – you must have heard about them. That's it. That's my story, more or less. Now can I order a coffee?'

O'Connor leaps to his feet but Hana beats him to it and makes him sit down again. She stands in line for her coffee and tries to breathe normally. Out of the corner of her eye she sees him settle down and stare out of the window.

Hana returns with her steaming double espresso and sets the cup carefully on the table. She looks up and meets O'Connor's stare.

'When we met I felt there was something strange about you,' he starts. 'Your face was ambiguous, your voice was ambiguous, and your suit looked odd on you.

But I couldn't go out on a limb and ask anything too personal, could I?'

She sips her coffee, head down.

'Anyway, at the time I knew nothing about the Kanun and northern Albania in general. It was the first time I'd set foot in the country, remember? Then I did a bit of research, I read a few things about it. I waited for you to call. I wanted to know how you had settled here in the US, but you never got in touch. I went back to Albania a few months ago. A couple of journalists in Tirana helped me try to find you, but . . . '

Hana smiles. She has finished her coffee and has nothing left to hide behind.

O'Connor is good-looking and relaxed, just as she remembers him. An oddball who's interested in strange countries like the Balkan states. This thought is a blow to her self-esteem. She called the wrong guy, she tells herself, panic rising.

'I'm really ashamed I called you,' she says, sincerely. 'I don't want to put you to any trouble. I'm a nobody to you.'

He lifts his hand.

'Tell me more, come on, and call me by my name. If I didn't want you to get in touch I wouldn't have given you my card. Let's just get the preliminaries and apologies over and done with, shall we? It's just ballast, right?'

'I've been thinking of calling you for months, but I was too scared,' Hana admits.

He smiles.

'We're just having a conversation here: your English is great and I'm all ears. What else do you need to help you relax?'

The bookstore café is beginning to empty and the bartenders at the coffee machine are no longer calling out orders.

'What if we get out of here?' O'Connor proposes. 'We could meet for dinner somewhere. You tell me where we can meet and –'

'I've made a mess,' Hana says. 'I wanted to see if someone who isn't Albanian can understand my story, but now I'm –'

'Regretting it,' O'Connor says, completing her sentence and laughing.

'Yes, regretting it.'

'Well, you did the right thing to call me,' he says, still trying to reassure her. 'But if you don't feel up to it . . . I won't insist. It's weird for me too. Things like this don't happen every day.'

They leave the café and the bookstore. Hana tells him that she came by bus that morning because her car is at the garage for an oil change. O'Connor offers her a lift, which she accepts so as not to be rude.

'My apartment is very modest and I don't feel comfortable letting you see it,' she hurries to add.

O'Connor assures her he has no intention of making her feel uncomfortable, and laughs again, shaking his head incredulously.

They climb into his Chrysler 300M and drive in silence until they get to Halpine, where Hana tells him to take a right.

'Right,' she says, trying to sound confident. 'I'll take a shower, put on the most elegant clothes I own and we'll go out to dinner. Is eight o'clock all right for you?'

The restaurant they have chosen is unpretentious and cozy. Sitting opposite him, she grins sheepishly and asks him to choose for her. O'Connor orders two prime ribs, jacket potatoes with sour cream, and green salad.

She stares out of the window. It's a beautiful May evening and there is blossom on the trees. She doesn't deserve this, she thinks. She doesn't know how to reconcile O'Connor, the grief she feels within her and can't expiate, and this incredible view.

'I don't know where to begin,' she opens.

For the first time, the thought flicks through her mind that maybe with Jack it would have been easier. She would have told him the story little by little, as if he were a kid in elementary school, and Jack would have said, 'No way!' He would have said he couldn't believe such a weird story. He would have said, 'Cool!' He would have said, 'You don't say?' But she never had the guts to tell Jack anything, maybe because he already has enough problems of his own, and he's black and their worlds seem so far apart.

Hana always felt her past would be too difficult for him to grasp. But she still feels guilty every time she thinks about Jack, and every time she runs into him.

Patrick O'Connor smiles, a little impatiently. Hana starts telling him about Gjergj, Katrina, her parents. She tells him again what a sworn virgin is, and goes through the various reasons why a woman might decide to become a man and give up any chance of life with a partner. As she finishes she flashes a smile at O'Connor, and tries to look as if what she has said is the most natural thing in the world.

The waiter, too chatty and obsequious for her taste, cracks a few stupid jokes as he brings their food to the table.

Now it's O'Connor's turn to be lost in thought. He cuts his meat slowly, mumbling 'Enjoy your meal' without looking at her. They eat in silence. She leaves half her ribs on her plate, and hardly touches her jacket potato. He finishes everything with evident pleasure.

'The fact that you're a woman who became a man . . .' O'Connor starts, setting his knife and fork straight on his plate. Hana puts her napkin down, then picks it up again and puts it on her lap. 'It's striking . . . Of course I'm curious, there's no doubt about that . . . and you know it too, right? Or you wouldn't have called me. A "sworn virgin." It's fascinating, yes.'

She tries to smile naturally, but doesn't feel she's succeeding. God, Americans are so direct, she thinks.

She likes this quality but at the same time finds it hard to deal with.

'Well, here I am, a living example, maybe the only one who has ever left the country. The others are all in Albania.'

She concentrates her attention on Patrick's hands. They're tanned. She asks him if he does any sport. He tells her about a little sailboat he shares with a friend and keeps in Chesapeake Bay.

She thinks that if she can make it to the end of this dinner without committing any major faux pas it'll be a miracle. O'Connor starts telling her a little more about himself. He lives alone. He makes a living as a freelance journalist for three print newspapers. He owns an apartment on Massachusetts Avenue. His ex-wife lives in Geneva and they are on good terms. No kids. No sentimental attachments since quite a while back. Has a hard time maintaining relationships owing to his job, which takes him around the world. A classic example of emotional failure, if that helps Hana feel more at ease.

She smiles shyly. She can see that his emotions are also playing tricks on him, and she's relieved. They start on the wine, which they had completely forgotten about.

'I thought you were gay, back when we were on the plane,' O'Connor confesses. 'Thanks for placing your trust in me.'

Hana sips her wine cautiously.

'Seriously, thanks. I must get hold of the Kanun and read it.'

Silence.

'You can read my story if you want,' Hana says.

O'Connor loosens his tie.

'In the years I lived as a man I kept a diary. I've re-written it here in my terrible English and my niece has corrected it – well, partly corrected it – so people can understand it.'

'Did you write any more poems?'

'I've been too busy taking care of myself,' she answers warily.

He lifts his arms, cocks his head to one side and smiles candidly.

'It's weird,' he says. 'I was sure I'd met people with the most tragic and unique stories. I have always traveled to their countries to seek them out: Nicaragua, Argentina, Lebanon, Pakistan, Bosnia. Yet now I'm here with you and I've just heard the most incredible story. You go around the world digging out stories and the real gem is sitting there right next to you. No cliché has ever been more true.'

He stops and thinks for a moment, then asks Hana about her family in Rockville. She tells him about Lila, Shtjefën, and especially about Jonida. She describes them in minute detail, and she tells him about how scared she is now that she has to manage her everyday life on her own after the months she spent at their house. A mountain girl like me, who'd never even seen a credit card, she tells him; she wasn't so sure she'd succeed.

She goes back to talk about Jonida, adding more stories. He listens attentively. Or maybe he's just developed the art of looking interested while his mind wanders over more distant pastures. He is a journalist, after all, Hana thinks.

'I'm talking too much, sorry.'

He takes her hand, as if to reassure her, and tightens his grip momentarily.

'No, I'm sorry,' he says. 'I'm still bowled over.'

He suggests going out for a short walk. Hana is embarrassed to say no. She's not used to this kind of thing, and it would be really nice to be taken home, she's pretty tired.

O'Connor gestures for the bill and then turns towards Hana, looking at her softly.

'I always take one step at a time,' Hana says. 'I don't know if you understand.'

'I'll take you home. But don't say we won't see one another again. I have a list of questions this long to ask you.'

'Slowly does it,' she says. 'I need time. Anyway, I don't expect anything from you. I don't expect any friendship. This meeting might be enough for me.'

'If we can't get away from this idea of obligation,' Patrick says, 'then we may as well forget the whole thing. All I'm offering is my pleasure in seeing you again, and understanding your story. It's up to you.'

On their way back to Hana's house, she stares out of the car window, wondering where she should put her hands, still resting in her lap for now. She lifts them and crosses her arms. That's better; she feels more in control. O'Connor is on Route 270, and politely waiting for her to speak first. But Hana feels more comfortable with silence. The evening is still glorious. Every building looks elegantly somber, the outlines of the trees in formation like guards on duty.

It's nice to be back in her studio apartment. Rockville is more than home. It's the perfect refuge for her quiet bewilderment.

Everyone is alone at the heart of the earth . . . [10] Her and the trees and the asphalt desecrated by the cars taking solitude out for a ride.

When he stops the car, he shakes her hand. Like a year and a half ago, as if he were saying goodbye to a man not a woman. She feels it. What is this? Are you flirting with him? she asks herself critically, as she goes up the stairs.

She can't sleep that night. She listens to the silence, staring at the ceiling. At around three in the morning she gets up and goes over to Nick, the computer, waiting on standby. She furiously types a page of disconnected thoughts and the process of writing arouses her. She feels she wants to touch herself, and she does so without any sense of shame. She plays with herself but she can't reach the peak of pleasure she feels is there waiting, and so she stops, tired out. She readjusts her summer pajamas. She apologizes to herself, turns Nick off, and goes back to bed, waiting for sleep that refuses to embrace her.

The next day, before going to the bookstore, she scribbles through the words 'Call O'Connor!' on the note in the kitchen, leaving only the exclamation mark, and goes out, whistling.

A few days later, Jonida is over at her place for the weekend. Hana gives her the lowdown on her dinner with O'Connor. Her niece is wearing pink pajamas from Victoria's Secret, with 'HOT' embroidered over her behind. The chest-hugging top is bright orange, with pink lace on the shoulder straps. Jonida's hair is bunched into two braids like Pippi Longstocking.

They've just finished eating. Hana made an Indian dish, basmati rice with eggplant, which she's very proud of. She's trying out recipes from around the world, with occasionally disastrous results. Jonida stares hard at her.

'Go on, tell me more. That can't be it. At least I hope it's not,' she pleads.

'Of course that's it. What else d'you want me to say?' Hana teases.

'You didn't tell me you were going to call him, though.'

'Yeah, right. You think I was going to say: "I have to call Patrick O'Connor"?'

'We promised we wouldn't hide anything from each other,' her niece objects. 'And now you're behaving just like Mom.'

'And how would that be?'

'She decides which promises she wants to keep.'

Hana clears away the plate of rice and gives Jonida a salad plate. She serves both of them. They've seen less of one another recently. Jonida is really busy at school, studying with ferocious determination and a genuine ambition to make something of her life.

For weeks at a time she is absent from the world of the three adults in her family. Lila is really upset about it. Shtjefën manages to stay close by playing basketball with her occasionally. They go out and shoot a few hoops and come back home arguing furiously. Her father says she fouls all the time and Jonida counters by saying her father's so short of breath he can't keep up with her anymore. She's strangely sure of herself for a teenager. She's unusual in that she's pragmatic and sensitive at the same time.

Hana watches her devour the salad. Once, she asked Lila how Jonida would have turned out if she'd grown up in the mountains back home. Lila answered straight off that her daughter would have got herself into deep trouble. She would never have accepted the rigid mentality and suffocating social control of the clan, and no way would she have accepted having to submit to a man. 'She's like you, Hana,' her cousin concluded.

Everyone comes to a conclusion. At the end of every sentence, there is a period. Nobody openly expresses perplexity or doubt. This is a typically American quality, she thinks. Hana doesn't like the idolatry of the winner, of the over-confident. Jack felt the same, though he worked his butt off trying to climb the social ladder, and always considered himself a failure.

Jack had recently found a new girlfriend. She was cute and quiet, from St Kitts, where his numerous family also came from.

'This is the honeymoon period, baby, then she'll probably leave me,' he would say to Hana, over and over. 'I've had plenty of experience of women changing their mind and leaving.'

Jack used to call her 'honey,' 'friend,' 'cutie.' He knew Hana spent her time writing.

'You want stories to write?' he asked her one day. They were at her house, a plate of spaghetti with meat sauce in front of them. 'I'll tell you the story of my family and you'll have plenty to write about.'

Hana answered that she had enough stories inside her to last two lives, not one. He disagreed and said she may have some harsh experiences to write about but they were nothing compared to those of the African Americans.

'So, my stories are about whites,' Hana argued, growing more irritated. 'Why is that supposed to matter?'

'It's just not the same thing, and it can't be more dramatic.'

'Jack, is this a competition about who has suffered the most now?'

'You can put it that way if you want.'

He had had a little to drink before getting to her apartment. He was drinking as he was speaking. He was particularly sad that day and Hana didn't dare ask why.

'Go tell your story to someone who can write, then,' she said, trying to bring the discussion to a close. 'I sell books and I read them. I don't write them.'

Jack reminded her that the fairytale Hana had invented for his daughter Taneea's birthday was beautiful.

'Why don't you want to hear my story, Hana?' he insisted.

'When I'm ready I'll tell you why.'

'Why are you so nervous today?'

'I don't know.'

But she did know. The fact was that Jack was generous and she wasn't. If Hana never got to know Jack's family's secrets, it would be easier for her never to let her demons out.

'You're some tough nut, you know,' Jack grumbled, as he went out onto the balcony to smoke a cigarette. After a while they called a truce.

'When are you bringing Gabrielle over to dinner? I'd like you to meet Lila and Shtjefën,' Hana said. 'We can do something more useful than telling each other our sob stories.'

Jack looked at her as if he were seeing her for the first time.

'Try understanding the first thing about you, cutie.'

Gabrielle, who was a professional nurse, would be able to encourage Lila to enroll in the nursing school. Her cousin was scared of making a wrong move. After speaking with Shtjefën, Hana wanted to help Lila make a decision, but she wanted to do it so discreetly that Lila wouldn't even notice.

'You're one big egotist, Hana Doda,' Jack had said. 'But I love you anyway.'

Jonida gets up from the table. She's finished her salad and she stares at Hana impatiently.

'If you go on just sitting there without saying anything, I'm out of here.'

'Sorry, I was somewhere else for a minute.'

Jonida pulls a face. Hana gets up too and thrusts her hands in her pockets.

'You're a nightmare,' she protests, laughing. 'You're always threatening me.'

'But it works, right? You were thinking about O'Connor, weren't you? Come on, tell me the truth.' Jonida takes a bottle of mineral water from the fridge.

'No, I wasn't. I was thinking about your mom being scared to go to nursing school, and about Jack. I swear. I wasn't thinking about Patrick.'

'Why? What's the big deal if you were thinking about him?'

'There's no big deal, but there's not much to think about either. He's just a journalist who's interested in the Balkans and who wanted to understand things, that's all.'

Jonida looks at her. She pauses to think, and a shadow of sadness crosses her face.

'A friend of mine's mom died yesterday,' she says, changing the subject. 'A heart attack. She'd never had any problems. She was, like, forty. She was really nice. I met her a few times at basketball games. She was a bit like Mom, you know. They're Italians, from Catania? Giovanni, my friend, he's going over there now to bury his mom.'

Hana mumbles something like 'I'm sorry,' which Jonida doesn't even hear.

'Well, I said to Mom and Dad, if there's one thing you must never do to me, it's die. Never never never.'

'What are you talking about?'

'And you too,' Jonida says, interrupting her. 'It's the same for you. Don't try playing some kind of fucked-up joke on me for at least a hundred years, do you hear me? I want you all here with me.'

'Jonida, love . . . '

'You're just not allowed, ok?'

She gets up, turns her back to Hana and starts washing the dishes.

Patrick O'Connor gets in touch in the first week of June. He gets right to the point and asks whether she'd like to meet him somewhere.

'I waited for you to call, as we agreed, but since you didn't, I decided to go against my word,' he says.

Hana is frying *qofte* and the pan is sizzling happily. The call makes her so nervous she turns the hot plate off and starts striding back and forth. She yearns for a cigarette; there's a pack she has kept hidden away – who knows why – in the bureau drawer. She lights one and takes a deep drag, feeling immediately giddy.

'Hana, are you still there?' Patrick says.

'You decided to waste your time on me?' Hana asks ironically, looking at herself in the mirror.

'So, when shall we meet?'

Hana opens her mouth wide in mute celebration, then she clears her voice.

'I'd prefer not to go to a restaurant this time,' she says, choosing her words carefully. 'You end up paying the bill and I can't even play the role of saying we can split it. It wouldn't be honest, because my finances are very – '

'I can add up,' O'Connor interrupts. 'I've lived in the US all my life. So, what do you suggest?'

'I don't want to come over to your place either.'

She moves out of the corridor to avoid the reflection of the mirror, which is making her nervous.

'It looks like there's nowhere in the world where we can meet and have a chat,' he jokes.

'If it's no big deal for you, why don't you come over to my place?' Hana says, surprising herself and immediately regretting her words.

O'Connor says he doesn't want to make things difficult for her. He'd like to see her but if every time it turns into a drama . . .

'So, would you come round here tonight?' She feels protected in her little apartment. 'I've made enough food for an army. I don't know why, I got the amounts wrong. Are you used to weird food?'

Whatever questions O'Connor decides to ask her, in her home she feels she can answer them.

Hana takes a shower and tries not to wet her hair. The day before, she went to the hairdresser and had her hair shaped around her small, well-formed ears. She puts on a push-up bra. She dresses in white, pants and a linen shirt. She looks good and she knows it.

Whatever happens that evening, as long as it doesn't turn into a vale of tears, she'll be ok, she thinks, as she prepares herself.

O'Connor is wearing a musky, powerful aftershave that lowers her defenses right away. He hands her a beautiful bunch of flowers and kisses her lightly on the cheeks. Hana has the impression that something is moving too fast, but he's just friendly, thoughtful, and a little cautious. He takes a seat, smiling at her. There's a long embarrassing pause. Then he confesses that he has read a lot about Albania in the past few weeks. He has read everything he could get his hands on. He even found the Kanun.

Hana doesn't know what to do about the dinner that is ready. Patrick shrugs his shoulders.

'I won't ask any questions if you don't want me to.'

Why is he sitting there? Why him?

'Why are you here, Patrick?' she asks suddenly, looking at the floor. 'It's all so unbalanced, the way I met you, my constant state of tension . . . ' She stops as suddenly as she started and doesn't know how to continue.

For a while now she's been unable to balance her thoughts out, and that makes her angry. It's weird but when she was Mark she was better with words. Mark weighed them out inside himself, observed and honed them, stroked them, at times erased them from his mind. As a man, silence was his ally. In silence there was hope; in conversations there often wasn't. Sound played for the enemy side. Once feelings were expressed, they lost their beauty, lost their color, and became diaphanous. The idea of beauty seems beyond her grasp now. Mark, Hana thinks, is the one who's kept his hold on beauty. In her haste to become the woman 'Hana,' she is losing something she can't quite put her finger on. Patrick's patience is also running out, she realizes.

'So, Hana?' he urges her on. 'Explain yourself better: what do you mean by what you were saying?'

She takes courage and looks up. She asks him brusquely why he wants to get to know her better.

'That sounds like an accusation,' he observes.

'Yes, I'm a bit defensive.'

'You're not very trusting.'

'Sorry.'

Patrick changes tack.

'I'm hungry, Hana. Did you forget you'd invited me to dinner? I didn't ask you to. Maybe if you give me some dinner, I'll feel better and then you can mistreat me as much as you like.'

She laughs. First point to him. She explains what she's about to bring to the table and Patrick says he'd eat a piece of rock served on a salad leaf. He has had a bad day and skipped lunch. The tension eases slowly. Hana serves her dishes on cream-colored plates. The tablecloth is green linen and looks good with the crockery.

She asked the guy in the liquor store to advise her about wines. He suggested a Californian Cabernet. She knows nothing about wine.

After a toast they eat in silence. Her guest wolfs down the *qofte* and vegetables, while Hana sips her wine. It's just so nice to have him there, sitting opposite her. She now feels strangely calm, and her movements become more harmonious and less spasmodic.

'I hardly dare say it's delicious because you'll surely say I'm only being polite,' Patrick teases. 'Can I have some more?'

He knows what he's doing, she thinks, serving him seconds. She feels her head spin. She closes her eyes. She's trying her utmost to keep her self-control, but she's not doing very well, so she may as well let go altogether. She drinks her wine in great gulps. She pushes her plate away and listens to O'Connor talk about his last two weeks, and the tragedy of his friend who was just diagnosed with cancer. She runs her hands through her hair, and goes on drinking. Patrick notices. He looks at the bottle and then at Hana's glass. He has drunk very little.

'I want you to stay,' she begs him. 'Just for tonight. For now,' she corrects herself. 'If you don't have the guts to deal with your shyness, you make a fool of yourself by drinking. And I've drunk quite a lot.'

He's about to say she's not making a fool of herself, but stops.

'Looking you up was a mistake, Patrick. I have no right to drag you into my mess, and now I'm panicking.'

He doesn't say a word.

Hana gets up and sways towards the bureau. She notices he's not looking at her, so as not to embarrass her. She lights a cigarette and takes a long drag. She turns around and offers her guest the pack. If she takes no notice of his disappointed expression, there may be some hope of recovering at least some of her dignity.

'I shouldn't have drunk anything,' she murmurs, sitting back down. 'I used to drink a lot. It was part of being a man, but you wouldn't understand that.'

'Yeah, right. I wouldn't understand because I'm American? Because I'm a man? Explain yourself. I might understand if you tried a bit harder.'

'It's too much for me. It would be too much for you.'

'Stop it. I'm fifty years old and I've been around a good while. You're not dragging me anywhere, I already told you.'

'Is it curiosity then? Is it that you feel you found a rare insect for your collection?' Hana stops, but it's too late.

She hears the sound of the train as it passes her house, metal screeching on metal, carriage after carriage. I've ruined everything, she thinks. Good thing too.

'I'm sorry, Patrick. I really am.'

'God, you really like saying sorry, don't you?'

'Are we having a fight?'

Hana feels shame riding up her throat. She bursts into tears and drops her head on the table. O'Connor doesn't move from his seat. It's like he isn't even there.

When she manages to calm down, she can hardly get up. She goes into the bathroom and rinses her face, then buries her face in the towel and rubs until it hurts. She drags herself into the bedroom and picks up a big folder full of papers.

She goes back into the sitting room and gives the whole wad to O'Connor.

'I owe you this at least,' she says, without looking at him. 'This is my story. When you've read it, you don't need to give it back to me in person. You can mail it. That way I can make up for putting you in this embarrassing situation.'

In the weeks that follow Hana throws herself into her work at the bookstore with fierce determination. Lila gets the message that it's best to give her space. Jonida is coming up to the end of her junior year at high school and has so many tests she has no time to come over.

Hana spends her evenings zapping aimlessly from one TV channel to another. She can't read, and she doesn't feel like her usual evening walks. In her overriding concern not to think about anything, one wish drills through her consciousness and hammers at her brain: that O'Connor mustn't get in touch. If he vanishes off the face of this earth, she'll be safe.

At the end of June, however, Hana receives a letter from Patrick, saying he's read her story. The whole thing, over and over, every detail. He won't be able to return her manuscript, though, until he gets back from a trip to the Baltics, where he's planning to stay for three weeks. He doesn't plan to send it back by mail. It's clear, he writes, that their relationship isn't going to take a normal course, but he needs and wants to give her the book back in person.

It's not a book, Hana thinks. It's just my life. It's just a life; books are different.

'I hope to see you when I get back,' he writes, 'and if this letter irritates you, deal with it.'

Hana gets up, puts the letter on the table, and goes out onto the balcony. Kids are playing in the square below, skipping or throwing balls, most speaking Spanish, others calling out in languages from around the world. Two young black mothers, holding newborn babies, keep an eye on their older kids, but Hana can't see who belongs to whom.

A month later, when they finally meet, Hana wears no makeup, although the week before she had highlights put in her hair.

They agreed on a stroll along the Potomac without too much haggling and, as they take the well-trodden path, Patrick tells her about his trip. Rowboats and kayaks slip along the river beside them. Having returned only the day before, Patrick is still jet-lagged, yet the conversation flows smoothly. Eight weeks have passed since their last, disastrous meeting. The neutrality of their surroundings clears the air.

Then Patrick abruptly changes tack, asking about Albania, the mountains, women's rights under the Kanun, and the dictatorship. She answers diligently, leaving nothing out.

They stop and sit on a bench, enjoying the river view and watching the Washingtonians thronging the park.

'Why did you do it, Hana?' Patrick asks, after a long silence. 'You never say why, in any of your diaries. From what I understood, your uncle would never have made you marry against your will. What you write about him doesn't explain why you took such a drastic decision.'

She looks him straight in the eye and answers honestly, not worrying about sounding melodramatic. Her gesture, she says, honored Gjergj Doda, and gave him a few more months of life and dignity. If he had forced her to marry, he would have known he had done something she hated and he would have died a sad man. And if she had disobeyed him, Gjergj Doda would have lost face. The mountains couldn't allow it. When Hana became a man, Gjergj died brimming with pride.

It was a gesture of love; perhaps it was also a delusion, Hana concedes, smiling and shaking her head. To start with she felt like a character in a play, like the heroine – no, the hero – of a popular novel. Then the feeling wore off, she admits, but by then it was too late, of course. Anyway, what was the point of regretting things up there in the cursed mountains?

She looks over at two squirrels fighting over an acorn. Patrick absorbs her words slowly. Then he takes her hand and shifts his body instinctively closer to her. She rests her head on his shoulder.

'Welcome to my life, Hana,' he murmurs. 'Whatever direction our friendship takes, you're in my life, and you are most welcome.'

Without another word, Patrick takes her home. In the car she stares ahead and says nothing. At her door, he kisses her forehead and leaves.

Hana stands completely still. She looks within herself, and is filled with nostalgia and happiness. She is rediscovering the Hana that used to be, the Hana who sat beside Gjergj Doda in his last hours, the Hana she has spent all these years trying to suffocate and forget.

She held the dying man's hand for four whole days.

'He's on his way out. He's more dead than alive, can't you see?' a doctor from the nearest town had said. 'Let him go. If you allow him to, he'll pass away this evening.'

Gjergj resisted for four more days, gripping Hana's hand desperately. It was his hand that held on, not him.

He would have let go sooner, but his hand wouldn't allow it.

When his grip loosened and his fingers went cold, she understood it was time to think about the funeral. She didn't look at his face. She got up and went to the bathroom. Her bladder had been killing her for the last three hours, but she hadn't dared take her hand away.

She squatted over the toilet and finally let go, staring at the wall in front of her. In the corner there was an ancient patch of mold; as a child she used to see the shapes of animals and people in it, as if it were a cloud.

She checked all the rooms in the *kulla* to see that everything was in order. Then she went back to her uncle's deathbed. Now she looked at him. She kissed him on the forehead. His eyes were closed, but he still did not have the color of death. Soon his skin would start to grow darker, she had heard.

You're free now, Hana, she told herself. You're done for.

It was five in the morning. Mark took the rifle off the wall and stepped out of the hut. He fired a few shots in the air to announce the death to the village.

In the days that follow, Hana can't stop thinking about the walk with Patrick along the Potomac. She has succeeded in having an almost normal conversation with a man, and the awe he inspired in her now feels like a fledgling sense of self-confidence.

After all, she's lived in the US now for a good year and a half, and she has made it. She hasn't had, and still doesn't have, the ability or the ambition to understand herself. That's another matter altogether. Putting together all the pieces of her puzzle: this was and is her project. While she eats her solitary dinners, she thinks with a certain pride of how far this project has taken her.

She had the balls to do it. They still hurt from the effort. She smiles at the paradox. She's made it on her own. That's all that counts. The rest, the world, can wait. She is Hana, the Hana of her stories and of the skirts that sit badly on her hips. The world outside can wait. Take your time, please.

She feels replete, a little dizzy without drinking a drop, crazy and wise. She sings out loud and strides around the apartment like a general.

'Get a grip,' she admonishes herself. 'And cut all this pride crap. Take it easy.'

She observes herself from the outside severely. 'Be normal, for God's sake.'

Nine days later, Patrick calls again. They decide to meet that evening. It is Monday. She has the morning shift at the bookstore so she has all the time in the world to get ready. She wants to be relaxed and in control of herself. She wants him to notice a change in her.

Even a relationship as weird as this one has its purpose, she tries to convince herself. The fact that she sought him out or that he wanted to listen wasn't such a prodigiously big thing after all. People continue to tell stories, thank God. And thank God some people continue to trust others and sometimes that trust is not betrayed. Hana steels herself: whatever Patrick has in mind for that evening, she is ready. Her newfound serenity will not be lost.

Now is the time to tell Lila why she's been lying low for the past few weeks. When Lila hears her voice she's overjoyed.

'I thought you had left town. I've missed you so much, I have a million things to tell you. I would have come over this evening anyway, I couldn't wait any longer.'

Hana tells her cousin she won't be home this evening so she had better tell her now. Lila talks as if a dam has opened. At the hospital where she has a cleaning job they said they could help her. They offered to fund part of her nursing course – only if she makes all her grades, of course.

'I have to fill in a pile of paperwork,' she says breathlessly.

Hana congratulates her. 'I told you you'd find a way.'

'The Human Resources manager says I have good potential,' Lila yells down the phone. 'Are you sure we can't meet this evening? What do you have on that's so important?'

Hana confesses she's going out to dinner with a man. Lila is struck dumb.

'What? A man?'

'I'm not going out with a monkey, if that's what you mean,' Hana answers, laughing. The floodgates open again and Lila gives her the third degree. To save time and effort, Hana feeds her the name Patrick.

'The guy with the business card? The journalist?'

'That's the one.'

'When did see him?'

'A few weeks ago.'

'A few – how many?'

'A couple of months ago.'

'You are evil, Hana Doda, you are a real . . . '

Hana hangs up on her before Lila goes into paroxysms.

Patrick hugs her tenderly and sensitively. He puts her hands together and holds them tight. He knows what he's doing; he wants to find the right way to handle her.

He says he'd just like to see her every now and then. Without stress. He'd like to spend time with her, as much as she wants. It's simple. To be friends without worrying whether there's anything unbalanced in the relationship.

She stares at him as he speaks without saying a word.

'So?' he laughs. 'You're not going to take weeks to answer, are you? I just want to clear up a few things. I'm not looking to have some kind of outlandish affair because that's not what you need.'

Hana has trouble mustering an appropriate response. She's panicking again, and she confesses as much. His response is perfectly sensible and that's why, in the days to come, she is sure she'll be wondering where the hitch is. She's not used to this. She doesn't believe in the perfect man. Not even in novels.

'How many women in the world . . . ' She leaves the sentence incomplete. Then she goes on, almost bitterly: 'There must be something wrong with you. You can't be perfect. Your perfection scares me – and it's irritating too.'

Patrick laughs. And the drop in tension helps her.

'Hana,' he says. 'I'm not desperate and I'm not trying to trick you into anything! Don't worry, I have plenty of defects. Perfect? Me?'

She tells him she's scared. Before he arrived, and in the last few days, she was calm. Now she's feeling nervous, so it's better if she doesn't say anything else, or she'll just talk garbage. He looks at her incredulously, but still with a twinkle of fun.

'Tell me the truth,' she pleads. 'You're regretting this now, right? I can see it. It's not a matter of regretting things, or being convinced about what we're doing.

I just know this isn't going to work. Pretending to be something I'm not, deceiving each other. It's no good. It can't work.'

Patrick gets up slowly and looks away. She follows closely behind. At the door she feels a sudden desire to curl up right inside him, but she doesn't let him read her thoughts. She lets him kiss her forehead while she kisses him all over in her mind.

'I'm sorry, Patrick. I've messed up again.'

He's already out of the door, shaking his head without a glance back at her. He gestures goodbye and runs down the stairs. He has left his bunch of flowers in the apartment.

You're fucked, Hana tells herself. You'll never learn. You're totally in the shit, ruined for life. All he did was ask you to be his friend and you acted like he was proposing till death do us part. God, you're such an idiot. Worse than last time getting drunk and all that. What the hell do you want from him?

The question is loaded, and she decides to give herself a break that evening, because she knows damn well what the answer is, and it fills her with embarrassment.

She dials Lila's number again. If she spends another minute thinking on her own she'll lose it, there and then.

'Lila, I like him too much.'

'Where is he?'

'I sent him away. I messed up.'

'You're crazy! Weren't you two going out to dinner? Why did you do that?'

'Because everything he says makes too much sense. Come over. I need you here.'

Two months later Hana gathers her courage and calls Patrick on his cell phone. It's the beginning of September and it's still warm.

She needs to apologize to him, she tells herself, and be forgiven. She suggests going out to a quiet restaurant in Georgetown on the canal, if he wants and if he has time.

After saying sorry to a passerby for bumping into him, Patrick says he accepts her apologies, but is still doubtful about the rest. 'What do we have to say to one another?'

She waits for more. He doesn't provide it.

It feels like a slap and it hurts. She swallows the pain.

'Patrick?'

'Yes?'

'Please.'

Silence.

'This evening I happen to be free. I hope that is ok with you because tomorrow I'm going out of town and I'll be away for a good while.'

She thanks him and hopes her voice does not betray

how relieved she is. She tells him she'll pick him up in her ridiculous car; that way there'll be nothing else to know about her. He'll have seen everything.

'I wish!' he exclaims. 'Ok, see you this evening.' Hana imagines his smile, sees it cracking his face with expectant amusement.

'And I'm paying,' she adds.

'Have you finished laying down conditions?'

The restaurant Hana has imagined for months that she would choose is perfect. They decide to sit outside on the patio rather than inside with the air conditioning. Soothing Celtic music plays in the background.

They order scallops, which are served in a thick white sauce.

Hana launches right into her apologies.

'I'm sorry for every time I've put you out with a question; I'm sorry about my reservations; I'm sorry about my doubts.'

O'Connor doesn't answer. He's tanned, she notices. He must have been out sailing.

Another couple sits at the table near them. Patrick looks at Hana tenderly.

'All we do is explain, reflect, argue. How about we try lightening up a little? How about changing the subject for once?'

Hana explains she's the opposite of the kind of woman Patrick must like.

'And what kind of woman would that be?'

'Gorgeous, well-educated, chic, poised.'

He doesn't give an inch. Hana decides to start eating her food. She thanks the defenseless bivalve drowning in the béchamel. It's delicious.

Hana knows how to be silent. She knows how not to die. She knows how to love. She knows how to write. But she doesn't know how to make love. And she doesn't know how to hate. Now she knows all these things about herself. She also knows things can't go on as they are. She says all this to Patrick with unusual calm.

'There are some things,' she says, 'you and I can't talk about and . . . ' she stops.

'You're forgetting I learned your story by rote,' he says, reassuring her. 'It's all written in your diaries.'

Patrick rests his chin on both hands.

'So let's go make love,' he says, as naturally as ever. 'Let's finish these damn scallops. You pay the bill, since you're so concerned about it. Nobody is stopping you. And we'll get out of here. Nobody is stopping us. Don't panic. I'm not asking you to marry me, to have kids, to commit yourself for eternity. Friends give each other a hand. So let's try making love, if you feel like it. Start with that and then see what happens with your life.'

Hana has gone red. She tries smiling at Patrick and succeeds, without feeling awkward.

'Normally friends don't go to bed, right?' she quips, scared to mess up again.

'Nothing is normal between us, so what's the problem?' he says, coming to her aid. 'Let's go, Hana. We're not having this tug of war just out of friendship. There's more to it. Shall we try and find out what there is? You decide. Are we going to talk about it all night, or shall we go? It's been a while since I last made love too, if you really want to know.'

'How come?'

Patrick doesn't answer. Before getting up he silently swills down the last of the wine in his glass.

'The bathroom is at the end on the left if you need it.'

Hana goes into the enormous room. She doesn't look around, she goes straight to the mirror. She sees herself reflected dressed in red, in a tight knitted skirt. She steps out without even rinsing her face, which is burning. Then she goes into the sitting room, where Patrick has lit a small table lamp and lots of candles.

He sits her down on the sofa and hugs her. Then he kisses her on her forehead.

•

Patrick's hands slowly stroke her nipples, then slide down towards her hips, where they come to rest. Hana takes a while before she lets herself go. He caresses and kisses her, while she tries to figure out whether she likes what he's doing. She's terrified of reciprocating his gestures, so she grabs hold of the sheet and feels safer.

'You're not drowning,' he whispers.

He realizes Hana is still not feeling much, so he moves down and gently opens the lips of her vagina with his tongue. He plays with her, teasing her clitoris, doing all those things she's seen in the films but this time she's beginning to sense the pleasure, then she feels it take her over. Patrick readjusts his body until the two forms fit together perfectly, and waits until she's ready before slowly sliding into her.

He carries on kissing her, warm and relaxed, happy even. Sitting up against the bedstead, he pulls her to him and she rests her head on his shoulder.

'It's been a year since I last made love.'

'And I'm free of this thing,' Hana says, amazed, smelling his skin and wondering what happens now. He hugs her closer.

'So?' he jokes. 'We're free of *this thing* together. Are you happy now?'

'How come you didn't make love for a year?'

He kisses her on the temple.

'I'll tell you another time, ok?'

Silence.

'But I didn't reach orgasm . . . '

'It'll happen. Next time we'll work on it.'

'It's not work,' Hana says, furrowing her brow.

'No, it's not. You're right.'

'Patrick?'

'Yes?'

'Did you like it?'

'I think so; I really think so.'

'Swear.'

'God, you talk a lot!' Patrick laughs, still holding her close, while Hana begins to feel awkward. She tries to free herself.

'Stay here,' he whispers. 'There's no hurry. There's absolutely no hurry.'

And he falls asleep.

She only pulls away from his embrace when Patrick's breathing becomes regular. She dresses and leaves his apartment. She drives home, concentrating fiercely on the road, and smokes the cigarette she has been saving for this *after*.

The night is deserted and strangely slow. But she is not at all. She feels alert and, as soon as she gets home, she has another smoke. Now she knows she has a life to live, whatever happens from now on. Before day comes, she'll sleep. Before any fear creeps back. She doesn't think it will. She hates her fear.

She has felt her body react; she felt it pulse.

'Welcome back, body,' she says out loud.

She throws her cigarette butt out of the window.

It's good to know she's alive.

AUTHOR'S ACKNOWLEDGMENTS

I am grateful beyond words to each and every person involved in the delicate process of shaping this story in translation from another language.

First to Clarissa Botsford: the deepest gratitude for loving my story in its original Italian, for deciding to translate it wonderfully at her own time and risk, and for her relentless search for a publisher. Clarissa's determination not to give up until she found one was my and this novel's good fortune.

I also extend grateful thanks to two other translators without whom *Sworn Virgin* would not be complete: Ruth Christie, who translated Nâzim Hikmet's poems from the Turkish, and John Hodgson, who translated Ismail Kadare's foreword from the Albanian.

I cannot thank And Other Stories and Stefan Tobler enough for believing in my novel – and indeed for being crazy enough to believe in literature in translation in the first place.

And a special thank you to Sophie Lewis for her meticulous work: I could not have dreamed of a better editor.

Elvira Dones

NOTES

1   *The vast, infinite life.* From part 1, section 8 of 'Quatrains' by Turkish poet Nâzim Hikmet, translated by Ruth Christie and Richard McKane (*Beyond the Walls*, Anvil Press, 2002).

2   *Goodbye, my brother sea.* From another poem by Nâzim Hikmet. A talisman text for Hana, lines from it recur in several places in *Sworn Virgin*.

Goodbye my Brother Sea

So we go as we came,
goodbye, my brother sea.
We took a few of your pebbles,
a little of your deep blue salt,
a little of your infinity,
a tiny bit of your light
and of your sorrow.

You told us many tales
of seafaring fate.
We have a little more hope
a little more courage.
So we go as we came,
goodbye, my brother sea.

(Translated by Ruth Christie, 2013)

3   *mixing Albanian Gheg with American English.* Gheg is the dialect
spoken in northern Albania.

4   *the* kulla *that was slowly going to ruin.* A typical stone-walled
'tower' house of the Albanian north, a *kulla* (plural: *kullë*) is
a family home that also functioned as a stronghold, with
narrow windows and thick walls.

5   *a Marubi portrait.* Pietro Marubi was an Italian painter and
early photographer who supported Garibaldi and emigrated
to Albania in 1850. Some of his portraits of Albanians were
published in the *London Illustrated News*.

6   *It's not a heart.* From another poem by Nâzim Hikmet:

Steamboat

It's not a heart, I say, it's a sandal of buffalo leather,
it tramps and tramps
        it never falls apart
                but treads the stony paths.

A steamboat passes in front of Varna,
'follow it, silver strings of the Black Sea,'
a boat on its way to the Bosphorus.
Nâzim caresses the boat very gently,
     and burns his hands . . .

(Translation by Ruth Christie, 2013)

7   *The* shilte *are in a mess on the floor. Shilte* are traditional mattresses or wide cushions for sitting or lying on.

8   *Don't you city people call us* malokë? A derogatory epithet suggesting mountain provincialism, roughly translatable as 'yokels.' Among the mountain folk themselves it can also be used as a term of endearment.

9   *the rule of the Kanun.* A set of traditional, orally transmitted Albanian laws, which were codified in the 15th century but only written and published in the 20th century. The Kanun remains a point of reference in the mountainous areas of north Albania.

10 *Everyone is alone at the heart of the earth.* From a poem by Italian poet Salvatore Quasimodo.

Suddenly It's Evening

Everyone is alone at the heart of the earth
pierced by a ray of sunlight:
and suddenly it's evening.

(Translation by Charles Guenther, in
The Sea and the Honeycomb, Beacon Press, 1971)

Dear readers,

We rely on subscriptions from people like you to tell these other stories – the types of stories most publishers consider too risky to take on.

Our subscribers don't just make the books physically happen. They also help us approach booksellers, because we can demonstrate that our books already have readers and fans. And they give us the security to publish in line with our values, which are collaborative, imaginative and 'shamelessly literary'.

All of our subscribers:

- receive a first-edition copy of each of the books they subscribe to
- are thanked by name at the end of these books
- are warmly invited to contribute to our plans and choice of future books

BECOME A SUBSCRIBER, OR GIVE A SUBSCRIPTION TO A FRIEND

Visit andotherstories.org/subscribe to become part of an alternative approach to publishing.

Subscriptions are:

£20 for two books per year

£35 for four books per year

£50 for six books per year

OTHER WAYS TO GET INVOLVED

If you'd like to know about upcoming events and reading groups (our foreign-language reading groups help us choose books to publish, for example) you can:

- join the mailing list at: andotherstories.org/join-us
- follow us on Twitter: @andothertweets
- join us on Facebook: facebook.com/AndOtherStoriesBooks
- follow our blog: Ampersand

This book was made possible thanks to the support of:

Abigail Miller
Adam Lenson
Adrian May
Ajay Sharma
Alan & Lynn
   Darragh
Alasdair Hutchison
Alasdair Thomson
Alastair Dickson
Alastair Gillespie
Alastair Kenny
Alastair Laing
Alec Begley
Alexandra Buchler
Alexandra de
   Scitivaux
Alexandra de
   Verseg-Roesch
Alex Martin
Alex Ramsey
Alex Read
Alex Webber & Andy
   Weir
Alice Brett
Alice Nightingale
Alice Toulmin
Ali Conway
Alisa Brookes
Ali Smith
Alison Hughes
Alison Layland
Alison Liddell
Alison Winston
Ali Usman

Allison Graham
Alyse Ceirante
Amanda Banham
Amanda Love
   Darragh
Amber Dowell
Amelia Ashton
Amy Capelin
Amy Sharrocks
Amy Webster
Ana Amália Alves
Andrea Davis
Andrea Reinacher
Andrew Marston
Andrew McCafferty
Andrew Nairn
Andrew Pattison
Andy Chick
Angela Creed
Angus MacDonald
Anna-Karin Palm
Anna-Maria Aurich
Annabel Gaskell
Anna Britten
Anna Holmwood
Annalise Pippard
Anna Milsom
Anna Vinegrad
Anne Carus
Anne de Freyman
Anne Marie Jackson
Anne Meadows
Anne Okotie

Annette Nugent
Annie McDermott
Ann McAllister
Anonymous
Anoushka Athique
Anthony Messenger
Anthony Quinn
Antony Pearce
Archie Davies
Averill Buchanan

Barbara Adair
Barbara Latham
Barbara Mellor
Bartolomiej Tyszka
Belinda Farrell
Benjamin Judge
Ben Schofield
Ben Smith
Ben Thornton
Ben Ticehurst
Bettina Debon
Bianca Jackson
Blanka Stoltz
Brendan Franich
Brendan McIntyre
Brenda Scott
Briallen Hopper
Bruce & Maggie
   Holmes
Bruce Ackers
Bruce Millar

C Baker
C Mieville
Camilla Cassidy
Candy Says Juju
    Sophie
Cara & Bali Haque
Carl Emery
Caroline Adie
Caroline Maldonado
Caroline Perry
Caroline Rigby
Carolyn A
    Schroeder
Carrie
    Dunham-LaGree
Carrie Love
Cath Drummond
Cecily Maude
Celine McKillion
Charles Beckett
Charles Fernyhough
Charles Lambert
Charles Rowley
Charlotte Holtam
Charlotte Middleton
Charlotte Morris
Charlotte Ryland
Charlotte Whittle
Chris Day
Chris Gribble
Chris Hemsley
Chris Lintott
Chris Radley
Chris Stevenson
Christina Baum

Christina
    MacSweeney
Christina Scholz
Christine Lovell
Christine Luker
Christopher Allen
Christopher Terry
Ciara Ní Riain
Ciarán Oman
Claire Brooksby
Claire C Riley
Claire Tranah
Claire Williams
Clare Lucas
Clarice Borges-Smith
Clarissa Botsford
Clifford Posner
Clive Bellingham
Clive Chapman
Colin Burrow
Cristopher Butler

Daisy
    Meyland-Smith
Damien Tuffnell
Daniela Steierberg
Daniel Barley
Daniel Carpenter
Daniel Gallimore
Daniel Hahn
Daniel Hugill
Daniel James Fraser
Daniel Lipscombe
Daniel Ng
Daniel Venn

Dan Pope
Dave Lander
David Archer
David Craig Hall
David Hebblethwaite
David Hedges
David
    Johnson-Davies
David Roberts
David Wardrop
Debbie Pinfold
Deborah Bygrave
Deborah Smith
Denis Stillewagt and
    Anca Fronescu
Diana Brighouse
Diarmuid Reil

E Jarnes
Eamonn Furey
Eddie Dick
Ed Tallent
Eileen Buttle
EJ Baker
Elaine Martel
Elaine Rassaby
Eleanor Maier
Elina Zicmane
Elizabeth Cochrane
Elizabeth Draper
Elizabeth Polonsky
Emily Jeremiah
Emily Rhodes
Emily Taylor
Emily Williams

Emma Bielecki
Emma Teale
Emma Timpany
Eric Langley
Erin Louttit
Eva Tobler-
    Zumstein
Ewan Tant

Fawzia Kane
Federay Holmes
Fiona Doepel
Fiona Malby
Fiona Quinn
Francesca Bray
Frances Perston
Francisco Vilhena
Francis Taylor
Fran Sanderson
Freya Carr

G Thrower
Gabriela Saldanha
Gabrielle Crockatt
Garry Wilson
Gary Debus
Gavin Collins
Gawain Espley
Genevra Richardson
Geoff Egerton
George McCaig
George Sandison &
    Daniela Laterza
George Savona
George Wilkinson

Georgia Panteli
Georgina Forwood
Geraldine Brodie
Gill Boag-Munroe
Gillian Cameron
Gillian Doherty
Gillian Jondorf
Gillian Spencer
Gina Dark
Gloria Sully
Gordon Cameron
Gordon Campbell
Gordon Mackechnie
Graham & Elizabeth
    Hardwick
Graham & Steph
    Parslow
Graham R Foster
Guy Haslam
Gwyn Wallace

Hannah Perret
Hanne Larsson
Hannes Heise
Harriet Gamper
Harriet Mossop
Harriet Sayer
Harrison Young
Helen Asquith
Helena Taylor
Helen Buck
Helen Collins
Helene Walters
Helen Weir
Helen Wormald

Henrike
    Laehnemann
Henry Hitchings
Hilary McPhee
Howdy Reisdorf
Hugh Buckingham

Ian Barnett
Ian McMillan
Ian Stephen
Inna Carson
Irene Mansfield
Isabel Costello
Isfahan Henderson
Isobel Dixon
Isobel Staniland

J Collins
Jack Brown
Jack Browne
Jacqueline Crooks
Jacqueline Haskell
Jacqueline
    Lademann
Jacqueline Taylor
Jade Yap
James Barlow
James Clark
James Cubbon
James Portlock
James Upton
Jane Brandon
Janet Mullarney
Janette Ryan
Jane Whiteley

Jane Woollard
Jasmine Dee Cooper
Jasmine Gideon
Jason Spencer
Jeffrey and Emily
  Alford
Jen Grainger
Jen Hamilton-Emery
Jenifer Logie
Jennifer Campbell
Jennifer Higgins
Jennifer Hurstfield
Jenny Diski
Jenny Newton
Jeremy Love
Jeremy Weinstock
Jerry Lynch
Jess Wood
Jim Boucherat
Joan Clinch
Joanna Ellis
Joanne Hart
Joe Gill
Joel Love
Jo Elvery
Johan Forsell
Johannes Georg Zipp
Jo Harding
John Conway
John Fisher
John Gent
John Griffiths
John Hodgson
John Kelly
John Nicholson

Jo Hope
Jonathan Evans
Jonathan Ruppin
Jonathan Shipley
Jonathan Watkiss
Jon Lindsay Miles
Jon Riches
Jorge Lopez de
  Luzuriaga
Joseph Cooney
Joy Tobler
JP Sanders
Judith Norton
Judy Kendall
Julian Duplain
Juliane Jarke
Julian I Phillippi
Julian Lomas
Julia Sutton
Julie Begon
Julie Freeborn
Julie Gibson
Juliet Swann
Julie Van Pelt
Juraj Janik

Kaarina Hollo
Kaitlin Olson
Kapka Kassabova
Karan Deep Singh
Kari Dickson
Katarina Trodden
Kate Gardner
Kate Griffin
Kate Leigh

Kate Pullinger
Kate Wild
Kate Young
Katharina Liehr
Katharine Robbins
Katherine Jacomb
Katherine Wootton
  Joyce
Kathryn Lewis
Kathy Owles
Katia Leloutre
Katie Martin
Katie Smith
Keith Alldritt
Keith Dunnett
Keith Walker
Kevin Acott
Kevin Brockmeier
Kevin Pino
KL Ee
Kristin Djuve
Krystalli Glyniadakis

Lana Selby
Lander Hawes
Larry Colbeck
Laura Bennett
Laura Jenkins
Laura McGloughlin
Laura Solon
Laura Woods
Lauren Hickey
Leanne Bass
Leeanne O'Neill
Leni Shilton

Lesley Lawn
Lesley Watters
Leslie Rose
Linda Broadbent
Linda Harte
Lindsey Ford
Liz Clifford
Liz Ketch
Liz Tunnicliffe
Liz Wilding
Loretta Platts
Lorna Bleach
Lorraine Curr
Louise Bongiovanni
Louise Rogers
Lucy Luke
Lucy North
Lyndsey Cockwell
Lynn Martin

M Manfre
Maeve Lambe
Maggie Humm
Maggie Peel
Maisie & Nick
    Carter
Malcolm Bourne
Malcolm Cotton
Mandy Boles
Mansur Quraishi
Marella Oppenheim
Margaret
    Duesenberry
Margaret E Briggs
Margaret Jull Costa

Maria Elisa
    Moorwood
Maria Potter
Marina Castledine
Marina Jones
Marina Lomunno
Marion Cole
Marion Tricoire
Mark Ainsbury
Mark Blacklock
Mark Howdle
Mark Richards
Mark Stevenson
Mark Waters
Marta Muntasell
Martha Nicholson
Martin Brampton
Martin Conneely
Martin Hollywood
Mary Ann Horgan
Mary Nash
Mary Wang
Mathias Enard
Matthew Bates
Matthew Francis
Matthew Lawrence
Matthew Shenton
Matt Oldfield
Maureen Cooper
Maureen Freely
Maxime
    Dargaud-Fons
Michael & Christine
    Thompson
Michael Harrison

Michael James
    Eastwood
Michael Johnston
Michael Kitto
Michael Thompson
Michelle Bailat-Jones
Michelle Purnell
Michelle Roberts
Michelle Roberts
Miles Visman
Milo Waterfield
Moë Faulkner
Monika Olsen
Morgan Lyons
Moshi Moshi
    Records
Murali Menon

N Jabinh
Nadine El-Hadi
Nancy Pile
Naomi Frisby
Nasser Hashmi
Natalie Brandweiner
Natalie Rope
Natalie Smith
Natalie Wardle
Natasha
    Soobramanien
Nathaniel Barber
Nia Emlyn-Jones
Nick Chapman
Nick Judd
Nick Nelson &
    Rachel Eley

Nick Sidwell
Nicola Cowan
Nicola Hart
Nina Alexandersen
Nina Power
Nora Gombos
Nuala Watt

Oladele Olajide
Olga Zilberbourg
Olivia Heal
Olja Knezevic
Omid Bagherli
Owen Booth

Paddy Maynes
Pamela Ritchie
Pat Crowe
Patricia Appleyard
Patricia Hill
Patrick Owen
Paul Bailey
Paul Dettman
Paul Gamble
Paul Hannon
Paul Jones
Paul Miller
Paul Munday
Paul Myatt
Paulo Santos Pinto
PD Evans
Peter Law
Peter Lawton
Peter Murray
Peter Rowland

Peter Vos
Philip Warren
Phyllis Reeve
Piet Van Bockstal
Pipa Clements
PM Goodman
Polly McLean

Rachel Bailey
Rachel Henderson
Rachel Kennedy
Rachel Van Riel
Rachel Watkins
Read MAW Books
Rebecca Atkinson
Rebecca Braun
Rebecca K Morrison
Rebecca Moss
Rebecca Rosenthal
Regina Liebl
Réjane Collard
Rhian Jones
Richard Dew
Richard Ellis
Richard Jackson
Richard Martin
Richard Smith
Richard Soundy
Richard Wales
Rishi Dastidar
Robert Delahunty
Robert Gillett
Robert Saunders
Robin Patterson
Robin Woodburn

Rob Jefferson-Brown
Rodolfo Barradas
Ronnie Troughton
Rory Sullivan
Rose Cole
Rosemary Rodwell
Rosie Hedger
Rosie Pinhorn
Ros Schwartz
Ross Macpherson
Ross Walker
Rufus Johnstone
Russell Logan
Ruth Clarke
Ruth Mullineux

SA Harwood
Sabine Griffiths
Sally Baker
Samantha Sabbar-
    ton-Wright
Samantha Sawers
Samantha Schnee
Sam Gallivan
Sam Ruddock
Sandie Guine
Sandra de Monte
Sandra Hall
Sara D'Arcy
Sarah Bourne
Sarah Butler
Sarah Nicholls
Sarah Pybus
Sarah Salmon
Sarah Salway

Sascha Feuchert
Sasha Dugdale
Saskia Restorick
Scott Morris
Sean Malone
Sean McGivern
Seini O'Connor
Selin Kocagoz
Sharon Evans
Shaun Whiteside
Shazea Quraishi
Sheridan Marshall
Sherine El-Sayed
Sian Christina
Sian O'Neill
Sigrun Hodne
Simon M Garrett
Simon Okotie
Simon Pare
Simon Thomson
SJ Bradley
Sonia McLintock
Sophie Johnstone
Stephen Bass
Stephen H Oakey
Stephen Pearsall
Steph Morris
Stewart McAbney
Stuart Condie
Sunil Samani
Susan Hind
Susan Murray
Susanna Jones
Susan Tomaselli
Susie Nicklin

Suzanne Smith
Swithun Cooper
Sylvie Zannier-Betts

Tammy Watchorn
Tamsin Ballard
Tamsin Walker
Tania Hershman
Tasmin Maitland
Tegwen Norris
The Mighty Douche
    Softball Team
Thees Spreckelsen
Thomas Fritz
Thomas Bell
Thomas Bourke
Thomas JD Gray
Tien Do
Tim Warren
Tim Theroux
Tim Gray
Timothy Harris
Tina Rotherham-
    Winqvist
Tina Andrews
Tom Mandall
Tom Bowden
Tom Darby
Tom Emmett
Tony & Joy
    Molyneaux
Torna Russel-Hills
Tracey Martin
Tracy Northup
Trevor Wald

Trevor Lewis
Tristan Burke

Val Challen
Vanessa Garden
Vanessa Nolan
Vasco Dones
Victoria Adams
Victoria Walker
Vinita Joseph
Visaly Muthusamy
Vivien Doornekamp-
    Glass

Walter Prando
Wendy Langridge
Wendy Toole
Wenna Price
Will Buck & Jo Luloff
William G Dennehy
William Prior

Yukiko Hiranuma

Zoe Brasier
Zoë Perry

Current & Upcoming Books by And Other Stories

Title: *Sworn Virgin*
Author: Elvira Dones
Editor: Sophie Lewis
Copy-editor: Bella Whittington
Proofreader: Alex Billington
Typesetter: Tetragon
Series & Cover Design: Joseph Harries
Format: B Format with French flaps
Paper: Munken LP Opaque 70/15 FSC
Printer: T J International Ltd, Padstow, Cornwall

FSC
www.fsc.org
MIX
Paper from
responsible sources
FSC® C013056